THE GOSPEL MAKERS

THE GOSPEL MAKERS

Anthea Fraser

St. Martin's Press ✥ New York

"A Thomas Dunne Book"

ISBN 0-312-13979-9

First published in Great Britain by Collins Crime,
an imprint of HarperCollins*Publishers*.

First U.S. Edition: February 1996
10 9 8 7 6 5 4 3 2 1

GREEN GROW THE RUSHES-O

I'll sing you one-O!
(Chorus) Green grow the rushes-O!
   What is your one-O?
One is one and all alone and evermore shall be so.

I'll sing you two-O!
(Chorus) Green grow the rushes-O!
   What are your two-O?
Two, two, the lily-white Boys, clothed all in green-O,
(Chorus) One is one and all alone and evermore shall be so.

I'll sing you three-O!
(Chorus) Green grow the rushes-O!
   What are your three-O?
Three, three, the Rivals,
(Chorus) Two, two, the lily-white Boys, clothed all in
green-O,
One is one and all alone and evermore shall be so.

Four for the Gospel makers.
Five for the Symbols at your door.
Six for the six proud Walkers.
Seven for the seven Stars in the sky.
Eight for the April Rainers.
Nine for the nine bright Shiners.
Ten for the ten Commandments.
Eleven for the Eleven that went up to Heaven.
Twelve for the twelve Apostles.

PROLOGUE

She wasn't to know those were the last words he would
ever say to her. Later, when she did know, she bitterly
regretted not having listened more closely. At the time,
though, she was concentrating on Celeste's birthday party,
to be held that afternoon.

It was one of those golden October days which, particularly in the Loire valley, one associated with the *vendange*.
As a child, she had helped pluck the grapes from her father's
vines, staining mouth and fingers with the rich ruby-red
juice. Best of all, she was allowed to sit with the *vendangeurs*
at the long trestle tables that lined the roadside while the
contents of huge tureens of soup, fragrant on the still air,
were ladled into bowls. The soup, the crusty *baguettes*, and
above all, the sweet, pervading smell of the grapes: these
were the memories that the word 'October' had conjured
up in her mind.

But never again. Instead, she would remember the sun-
filled kitchen and herself stirring the cake mixture in the
blue and white bowl, and Philippe lifting her hair to kiss
the back of her neck as he always did, and making some
comment about his trip to England. But she wasn't really
listening, because there were so many things she must do
before Celeste and her friends arrived back from school,
and because anyway he would tell her all about it when he
came back in four days' time.

How could she know he would not come back, ever
again?

CHAPTER 1

Detective Inspector Nina Petrie let herself into the house and leant against the door, pushing it shut behind her. Its warmth enfolded her, welcome after the cool afternoon air.

'I'm home!' she called.

There were simultaneous responses—from her eight-year-old daughter upstairs: 'Down in a minute, Mummy!'—and from her mother in the kitchen: 'The kettle's on.'

Nina smiled, propping her briefcase against the hall table. It was working well, this return to Shillingham. Her marriage breakdown a couple of years ago had coincided with her mother's deteriorating health, and when her promotion came up it had seemed sensible to opt to move back here. It was to their mutual advantage; her mother had company, and there was someone in the house when Alice came home from school or when, as increasingly happened, Nina was called out at night. Also, now that the initial prickliness with the DCI had been smoothed over, she enjoyed her job: far more challenging in this busy division than it had been in sleepy Oxbury.

She pushed open the kitchen door and her mother turned to greet her, teapot in hand. 'How did it go?'

'Like a dream. After four weeks' slog the case is wrapped up, and I've a free weekend ahead of me.'

'About time you had a chance to relax,' Mrs Paxton commented.

In fact, though, she was not yet ready to unwind; still exhilarated by the case, she felt restless, needing to do something positive, to go out somewhere, meet people. But since she'd no plans, the prospect of an evening's television, though boring, seemed inevitable.

There was a crumpled sheet of paper on the table and she picked it up. 'What's this?'

'Someone pushed it into my hand in Duke Street. I stuffed it in my pocket and forgot about it.'

'*Lonely? Restless? Dissatisfied?*' Nina read aloud. '*Does the future seem bleak? It needn't be! Don't miss this chance to change your life for the better! Everyone welcome TONIGHT, 5, Victoria Drive at 8 o'clock.*'

At the top of the sheet was a smudged logo of what looked like a triangle with a curved line above it. Nina frowned and flipped the paper over, but the back was blank. 'Isn't this the new cult everyone's talking about? The Revelationists or something?'

'Never heard of them,' Mrs Paxton said absently. 'Drop it in the bin, dear, tea's ready.'

Nina tapped the paper thoughtfully. 'They warned us at the station about this lot. They're not nearly as innocuous as they seem.'

Alice came running into the room and flung her arms round her mother's waist. 'I've finished my homework. We didn't have much today.'

'Good for you,' Nina said, patting the shining head. Then, to the older woman. 'You know, Mum, I think I might just go along.'

Mrs Paxton turned sharply. 'To the meeting? Are you mad? They'll brainwash you—that's how they get converts—turn you into a zombie, no good to yourself or anyone else. Nina, for pity's sake be sensible. You said they were dangerous. Throw that away and forget it.'

'But it's an ideal chance to see them in operation. It could be useful if there's trouble—and there's likely to be, sooner or later. Parents complaining their kids have been alienated, and so on.' She glanced at her own daughter, standing on one leg as she opened the biscuit tin. 'If we can prevent that, surely it's worth giving up an evening to suss it out?'

'But once you're there you mightn't get away,' Mrs Paxton said worriedly. 'They're manipulators, these people. There must be safer ways of keeping an eye on them.'

'Mum, I promise I'll be careful. I know what I'm walking

into, unlike the other poor devils who go along. And if I'm
not home by ten-thirty, you can call the fire brigade!'

Dilys Hayward stood in her study fighting down a growing
feeling of dismay as the voice of her god-daughter, blithe
and supremely unconcerned, came over the telephone.

'They won't be any trouble, darling, honestly. Seb's an
angelic baby and Sarah's highly trained and efficient.
What's more, she adores him, so you needn't worry on that
score. And the chance to go with James really is too good
to miss. I'd have asked the parents, but as luck would have
it they're in France at the moment, buying a house.'

Susie paused for breath and Dilys realized with a sinking
heart that she must make some comment. But, heaven
knew, the *last* thing she wanted at the moment was anyone
staying in the house—least of all a nine-month-old baby.
Her latest book was proving more difficult than anticipated
and she had a fast-approaching deadline.

'Susie dear, I really do think—'

'You needn't do a *thing*, darling, honestly! And as Sarah
prepares his feeds and does the washing, it won't affect
Peggy either.'

'You see,' Dilys put in feebly, 'I'm in the middle of a
book, and I really do need—'

'When you're tucked away in your study you'll hardly
know they're there, I *promise!* And it's only for three weeks,
after all.' Susie paused, then tried another tack. 'James is
always swanning off to somewhere fabulous, but this is the
first time I've been invited. If I turn it down they mightn't
ask me again. And I've always wanted to see Japan.'

Dilys, sensing she was beaten, made one final attempt.
'Why not take Sebastian with you?'

'To *Japan?*'

It wasn't Outer Mongolia, her godmother thought wasp-
ishly. But what was the use? 'When are you going?' she
asked, realizing even as she spoke that she'd accepted the
inevitable.

Susie's voice brightened. 'Next Tuesday, the twelfth.

You'll take them, then? Oh darling, you're a brick! What would I do without you?'

'Stay at home!' Dilys retorted incontrovertibly. 'But if they disturb my writing, I shan't be responsible for the consequences.'

She put down the phone and stood for a moment, her hand still on the receiver. 'Bloody hell!' she said, clearly and with emphasis.

She sighed, looking round the room that was her refuge, the centre of her universe. Within these walls had come to life the characters who'd won her major awards and played out their destiny on television screens across the world. Many was the night she'd spent on that faded sofa, feet tucked beneath her, scribbling in the lined notebooks which had preceded the word-processor.

The desk had been her father's, and was massive enough to accommodate with ease computer, printer and all the other accoutrements of her craft. Behind it, a window gave on to the side of the house where, bathed in the mellow sunlight of an October afternoon, the old walnut tree stood against the faded brick wall.

And, if the ideas didn't come, French doors leading to the garden provided an escape route. Although, Dilys reflected gloomily, for the next few weeks that sanctuary would be shared with a baby in a pram.

With a sense of impending martyrdom she walked through the adjoining sitting-room to the hall. In the dining-room opposite she could see Peggy, her housekeeper, laying the table for dinner.

'That was Susie on the phone. Her husband's giving a lecture at Tokyo University and she's been invited to go with him. They intend to stay on and make a holiday of it.'

'That's nice,' Peggy said comfortably, continuing to arrange the place-settings.

'What *isn't* so nice is that she wants to dump the baby and his nanny on us. For three weeks, heaven help us.'

Peggy straightened and looked across at her. 'Oh dear.'

'Precisely. Oh dear. I did my best to put her off, but her parents are in France and if I hadn't agreed it would have meant she couldn't go, which seemed a bit selfish.'

'But what about your book?'

'She insists I'll hardly know they're here. Nor will you,' she added, before Peggy could voice doubts on her own account. 'The nanny'll see to all the baby's food and washing.'

'Where will she sit in the evenings?' Peggy asked, unerringly pinpointing what to her was the major consideration. 'With us or with you?'

'Damn—I never thought of that.' Peggy and her husband had their own sitting-room off the back hall. 'I'll ask Susie what the form is. I don't know anything about the girl other than that she's fully trained and adores the baby.'

Peggy made no comment except, after a moment, 'What time do you want dinner?'

Dilys wrenched her mind from the problem which had so unexpectedly been thrust upon her. 'About eight-fifteen, I suppose—Hannah's due at seven-thirty. You'll remember to take the cheese out of the fridge, won't you?' She glanced at her watch. Six o'clock. No chance of any more work this evening. 'I might as well go and have my bath.'

'When are they coming, the nanny and baby?' Peggy called after her.

'Next Tuesday.' Oh, *why* had she let herself be talked into this, Dilys thought irritably. But it was too late to retract now. She could only hope Susie's confidence was not misplaced.

Nina had been standing on the corner of Lethbridge Road and Victoria Drive for fifteen minutes, and was glad of the warm anorak and trousers she'd changed into. From where she stood No. 5 was plainly visible, a tall Victorian villa no different from its neighbours, except that lights shone from every window.

During that time a steady trickle of people had turned into the road and made their way to the house. Each one had paused momentarily at the gate, as though wondering whether to change his or her mind and go home. But while Nina watched, no one did. One after another they went bravely up the path and were admitted to the house—by whom, she could not see. She glanced at her watch. Nearly five to eight—time to make a move herself.

She reached the gate at the same time as another woman, approaching from the opposite direction. They exchanged hesitant smiles and Nina followed her up the path to the front door. It was opened by a young woman.

'How nice to see you!' she said warmly, as though they were old friends. 'Come in—everyone's just getting to know each other. There's tea, coffee and soft drinks in the room down the hall. Mattie'll introduce you. Let me take your coats.'

At the top of the stairs, out of view of the group below, Adam Reed stood listening. Good for Sarah, striking just the right note as usual. A pity she wasn't one of the residents. Still, she'd be just up the road for the next three weeks while her employers were away. 'Seb and I are being sent to Mrs Trent's godmother,' she'd told him earlier that evening. 'She's a writer, and Mrs T stressed that she mustn't be disturbed, so with luck I'll have a fairly free rein. Should get a lot of useful work done.

'The phone's ex-directory, but I'll give you the number as soon as I know it. And if you do need to ring, don't forget you're my cousin. It saves explanations.'

He smiled wryly, regretting the small deceit and, even more, the reason for it.

From the common-room below the subdued murmur of voices reached him, as strangers shyly responded to proddings to introduce themselves. Daniel and Mattie would be there, greeting, reassuring. He should be with them, but tonight he was in charge of the meeting and, as always, assailed by nerves.

Within the space of little more than an hour, he had to try to save the lost souls who'd responded to their invitation.

Suppose he couldn't reach them? Suppose the possible converts slipped through his hands?

He drew an uneven breath. The sin of pride again—he'd
been warned of it. He must keep reminding himself that he
was only the mouthpiece, the channel through which the
power flowed. If the evening was a success, if they came
back, these newcomers, it would not be because of anything
he had done, but because the Captain had reached them
through him—the Captain and, of course, God.

Balance precariously restored, Adam started slowly
down the stairs.

'It has been brought home to me, Hannah,' Dilys commented, dropping a piece of ice into the glass, 'that I'm a
very selfish person. My world revolves entirely round my
own affairs, and I resent its being disrupted. If it had been
anyone but Susie I'd never have considered it.'

Hannah James took the glass from her. She knew how
adept Susie was at getting her own way; ten years ago she'd
been at Ashbourne School for Girls, where Hannah was
deputy head. 'I think it's very noble of you. Especially
since—' she hesitated.

'I'm not fond of babies at the best of times? Quite right.
They're only bearable when they're asleep and—most
importantly—someone else's responsibility.'

'Well, he will be, won't he? You don't have to get
involved.'

'All the same, I wish to heaven I'd said no.'

Hannah studied her friend's face, noting the signs of
stress. 'Is the book still heavy going?' she asked astutely.

Dilys grimaced. 'As you know, once I start I usually
sail through them, but this one's the very devil. And the
manuscript's due at the end of next month.'

'You'll do it,' Hannah said soothingly.

'I'm beginning to wonder. Still, enough of my problems—how are you getting on? Have you heard from
Gwen?'

Gwen Rutherford, headmistress of Ashbourne, was on a

year's sabbatical in Canada, leaving Hannah temporarily in charge.

'Yes, she's having a marvellous time. I had a long letter yesterday.'

'You know, I can never get used to the idea of you two as the Powers That Be. You bear precious little resemblance to the Powers That Were in our day, the Misses Payne and Didcot of blessed memory.'

Hannah smiled. 'That's a relief; though I've a lot more sympathy for them now.'

'Problems?'

She shrugged. 'It's early days—I'm barely half a term into my stewardship.'

Dilys regarded her shrewdly. 'All the same, something's worrying you. Not an outbreak of the dreaded Shillingham lurgy?'

'No, but there's a member of staff I'm rather concerned about.'

'Why's that?'

'Oh, just that she's living on her nerves. I was watching her at lunch the other day—she hardly ate a thing. And she dresses so oddly,' Hannah went on, warming to her theme. 'Her clothes are ancient and don't even fit—they're obviously second-hand. Honestly, to look at her you'd think she was on the breadline, yet she gets a decent salary and has no dependants that I know of.' She sighed. 'The last thing I want is to hurt her feelings, but I'll have to have a word with her. She's letting the school down and setting a bad example to the girls.'

'What's her subject?'

'English, and she's brilliant at it—a natural teacher. She gets quite exceptional results.'

'How long has she been with you?' Dilys asked, refilling Hannah's glass.

'A year now.'

'Why haven't you tackled her before?'

'It wasn't so noticeable at first—she merely looked eccentric. Now—well, she's like a down-and-out!'

'Perhaps she's taken up gambling?'

'Doubtful—it wouldn't be at all in character.'

'Has she a friend you could sound out?'

'Unfortunately no, she keeps her own company.'

A knock on the door announced dinner, and Hannah was glad to let the subject drop.

'I do love this house,' she remarked as they went into the dining-room. 'How old did you say it was?'

'It was built in the sixteen-sixties,' Dilys replied, gesturing for her to seat herself at the rosewood table, 'by a retired clergyman of private means. Hence the name "Hassocks".'

'I assumed it was because of those low, rounded bushes by the front door.'

'No doubt he was the first to plant them. Then, of course, bits and pieces have been added over the years, resulting in the hotchpotch it is now. I ask you, two halls and two staircases in a house this size!'

'Well, however it "growed", it's full of character, which modern flats simply don't have.'

'Yours has,' Dilys said. 'I envy you its space and stillness. Here, let's face it, everything's rather cluttered.'

Hannah watched her pour the wine. 'I've often thought you have the perfect life; a gorgeous house, someone to run it for you and a really satisfying career.'

'And no husband to put a spanner in the works!' Dilys finished for her.

'You don't regret that?'

'Occasionally, but he'd have to be a paragon to satisfy me. Someone who'd agree to live here—because I've no intention of moving—but not intrude on my privacy and never, never interrupt me when I'm writing.' She burst out laughing. 'I told you I was selfish!'

Hannah smiled noncommittally. There had been men in Dilys's life, she knew, some more important than others, but none of the relationships had come to anything. Close friends though they were, it was an area of each others' lives into which they never pried.

For many years there had been four of them—herself

and Dilys, Gwen, and Monica Tovey— all ex-Ashbourne pupils, all successful, unmarried women. They used to meet once a month, at the theatre or for dinner at each other's houses, and very pleasant it had been. Then, a few months ago, Monica had belatedly married, and soon after Gwen left for Canada. The ripples caused by both events had unsettled Hannah and, she suspected, Dilys also. For the moment at least, there were only the two of them.

'Peggy's excelled herself with this mousse,' she commented, laying down her spoon with regret.

'Yes, I never cease to bless Mother for sending her on that cookery course. It's paid dividends ever since.'

At the time of her mother's death, Dilys was just down from Oxford and looking for a home of her own, deterred only by a pathological dislike of housework. It had seemed a natural solution that she should inherit Peggy.

The arrangement worked admirably—so much so that when Peggy had married a few years later, her husband Bob was happy to move into Hassocks with her. He worked at the bus depot, but was more than willing to keep the garden in order and do odd jobs around the house in return for his board.

'You're right!' Dilys said suddenly, breaking into Hannah's reflections. 'I *am* lucky, and goodness knows I do little enough in return. It's time I put myself out for someone.'

Hannah forbore from pointing out that in fact she'd be put out very little. 'Good for you!' she said stoutly, and they settled down to enjoy the rest of their meal.

It was hot and crowded in the back room, and at regular intervals someone struggled through the throng with a tray and the repetitive query, 'Tea, coffee or squash?'

For the third time Nina politely declined, and for the third time found herself having to resist a more pressing invitation. 'Oh, do take one. It helps to break the ice.'

She smiled and shook her head, seemingly the only one present without a cup in her hand. In strange surroundings,

she told herself, it was prudent to eat or drink nothing—
not even six pomegranate seeds. The fancy amused her,
proof that her mother's warning had taken root.

As best she could in the cramped surroundings, she'd
been taking stock of her companions. There must have been
about forty of them, all obviously nervous, though, encouraged by their constantly smiling hosts, they had begun to
chat among themselves, exchanging names and occupa-
tions. Why had they come here this evening, she wondered.
What were they hoping to find? Surely they couldn't *all* be
'lonely, restless or dissatisfied?' Surely some, like herself,
were merely curious? She hoped so.

There seemed a roughly equal number of men and
women, and a surprisingly wide age range. Catching sight
of a couple of girls not far from her, Nina felt a twinge of
unease. They must still be at school. Did their parents know
they were here?

She studied them more closely. The fairer one, her yellow
curls in the fashionable untidy mop, was tall, slim and
extremely pretty. Her companion, though probably the
same age, was much shorter and her bushy hair framed a
small, piquant face out of which dark eyes glittered almost
feverishly from beneath heavy brows. Nina wondered how
old they were; fifteen, sixteen? A vulnerable age in this
place. She resolved to keep an eye on them.

A voice interrupted her survey. 'You've nothing to drink.
Let me get you—'

'Really, no! Thank you,' she added, trying to temper her
over-firm refusal. She turned to see a man of about her own
age smiling down at her.

'Fair enough,' he said easily, and she felt some of her
qualms subside.

'I'm Daniel,' he went on, shaking her hand. 'And
you're—?'

'Nina.'

'Delighted to meet you, Nina.' He took her elbow and
led her over to the wall, out of the crush. 'Tell me about
yourself. What do you do?'

She was ready for that one. 'I'm a civil servant.'

'Ah, one of the faceless millions! I know the feeling. Married?' He glanced down at the wedding ring which, to ward off advances, she still wore.

'Divorced,' she answered, and was taken aback by the swift, brief pressure of his hand.

'Well, you're among friends now. You need never feel lonely again.'

The comfort in that spontaneous gesture took her by surprise. She was as green as the rest of them, she thought, mortified. If this expert sales pitch could make her, guarded and suspicious as she was, feel warmed and wanted, what hope had the rest of them of escaping the net which, she had no doubt, would shortly close over them?

Stephanie French glanced at her watch. They seemed to have been here a long time without much happening, and her head was beginning to ache. She took another sip of squash, spilling it down her blouse as Marina suddenly clutched her arm.

'Steph—there's Miss Hendrix! Look, over there!'

Stephanie turned in the direction of her pointing finger, but the crowd was constantly shifting and she recognized no one. 'It can't have been,' she said positively.

'I tell you it *was*. Who else looks like Henny?'

Stephanie narrowed her eyes. Marina's face seemed a long way away and she was finding it hard to concentrate on what she was saying. 'Suppose she saw us?'

'So what?' Marina retorted defiantly. 'She can't report us without giving away that she was here herself. Anyway, we're not doing anything wrong.'

'I wish they'd say what it's about,' Stephanie complained. 'It'll probably turn out to be some boring old political party.'

'Or a high-powered dating agency! Still, it doesn't really matter, does it? It's better than sitting at home watching telly.' And trying not to hear raised voices in the kitchen, she added silently.

She pushed back the dark mass of her hair. 'I'm glad I saw that notice. Everyone here's so friendly. Even though we don't know them I feel sort of *fond* of them, as though we're all somehow in the same boat.'

'Me too,' Stephanie agreed. There was a sudden, perceptible movement towards the door, and she added, 'At last— something's happening. Now perhaps we'll find out what's going on.'

CHAPTER 2

Thank God it was Friday, thought Edward French, weaving his way expertly through the heavy traffic. He'd open a bottle of wine when he got home and they could enjoy a long, leisurely meal, with no meetings for either of them to rush off to. And later, replete and content, they would make love.

He waited at the traffic lights while a giggling group of schoolgirls, clutching each other's arms, hurried across the road. Oh God! he thought suddenly, his enjoyable anticipation deflating, wasn't this Stephie's *exeat* weekend? Christina had mentioned it the other evening; she'd arranged to fly up to Scotland on Saturday to meet a potential client, but, inclination conflicting as it so often did with duty, was wondering if she should cancel the trip.

'It's the limit, isn't it?' he'd remarked humorously. 'You pay an extortionate amount to have your children taken off your hands, and what happens? They're sent home at regular intervals to give the staff a break!'

'It wouldn't be so bad if they coincided,' she'd replied, 'but we seem to have one or other of them every few weeks. I had to postpone the Paris trip because Ned was home, and now it's Stephie. How can I run a business under these conditions?'

She was the proprietor of an interior design company, an enterprise which made full use of both her artistic flair and her business acumen. After an uncertain start it was just beginning to establish itself, with some lucrative business deals as well as a growing number of private clients.

'I should go if I were you,' he'd advised her. 'Stephie's not a child, she can amuse herself.'

'Will you be around?'

'Not a great deal, I'm afraid. This golf competition will take up most of the weekend.'

'It seems unfair to go off and leave her,' Christina said hesitantly. He'd waited, aware the decision had been taken and wondering how she'd justify it. 'On the other hand, I can't get out of that meeting with Mr Bryant—he's only here for the weekend. And anyway,' she'd added, salving her conscience, 'she'll probably spend most of her time with Marina, so it won't make much difference if I'm here or not.'

The lights changed and with a sigh Edward restarted the car. But when he arrived home minutes later there was no sign of his daughter. Christina was alone in the kitchen, preparing dinner.

'Where's our weekend visitor?' he asked.

'Out with Marina.'

To his shame, a tide of relief washed over him. 'Out where?' he asked, to disguise it.

She shrugged. 'You know Stephie—vagueness personified. A disco, I suppose. It usually is. Anyway, I told her to be back by eleven and to phone if she needed collecting.'

'So we can have our evening à deux after all,' he said happily, slipping his arms round her. She smiled and lifted her face for his kiss and Edward, as much in love with her as he'd been twenty-odd years ago, wondered not for the first time whether they'd done right to have children. They were fond enough of them, but in truth they'd have been as happy simply with their work and each other.

'Stephie wanted Marina to come for the weekend,' Christina commented, returning to her basting, 'but her parents wouldn't let her.'

'Why ever not?'

'Trying to play Happy Families, I suppose. Stephie says Marina dreads going home; Gordon and Diane spend all their time shouting at each other and trying to get her and Peter to take sides.'

'Things are no better, then?'

She shook her head. 'You saw him yourself, didn't you, with some woman? If you ask me, divorce is only a matter of time.'

'Poor devils,' Edward said, 'and poor kids, too.' Secure in his happy marriage, it never occurred to him that his own children, for quite different reasons, might also find the atmosphere at home less than welcoming.

As Nina moved with the crowd into the hall she found herself next to the woman who'd arrived at the same time as she had.

'You're by yourself too, aren't you?' she said shyly. 'Would you mind if I sat with you? To be honest, I'm a bit apprehensive.'

'I think we all are. My name's Nina.'

'Pam.'

They made their way back up the hall and through a door on the right. Double doors halfway down the room had been pushed back, opening what were normally two rooms into one large one, now set out with rows of chairs. At the far end was a dais with two chairs to each side of it and, at the back, a large screen. A projector had been set up level with the front row of chairs.

'Have you any idea what it's about?' Pam whispered, as she and Nina seated themselves.

'One of the New Age religions, I imagine.'

'That's what I thought. They seem very friendly.'

No doubt because they regarded Pam as a likely catch, Nina told herself uncharitably. She was a faded woman with fair, greying hair and little make-up, and kept twisting her wedding ring nervously round her finger.

Catching Nina's eye on it, she said ruefully, 'My old man

would scalp me if he knew I was here. How about yours?'

'I'm divorced,' Nina said. 'Why wouldn't he approve?'

'He thinks they're a right bunch of charlatans. Not only this lot, the regular crowd at St Martin's as well. Can't understand anyone still believing in religion—says we should have outgrown it years ago.'

'The opium of the people?' Nina suggested.

'What?'

'Like a comfort blanket.'

'Yes, that's it exactly. But we need a bit of comfort, don't we? I know I do.'

Everyone had now been seated, and there were not many empty chairs. A good turn-out, Nina thought cynically. Some of those who had been handing round drinks were now taking up strategic positions, one at the light switches, another by the projector. Then two men and two women came in together and walked down the length of the room to the dais. Nina recognized a couple of them, the man who'd spoken to her, Daniel, and the woman who'd greeted them at the door. They took their seats to the left of the dais, the other two to the right. Then, as an expectant hush descended over the room, the other man stood up again and moved to the front of the stage. Surreptitiously Nina switched on the concealed microphone in her button-hole.

'Good evening, everyone, and welcome. We're delighted you could come. My name is Adam and my friends here are Mattie'—he gestured to the odd-looking woman behind him—'Sarah and Daniel.'

Nina settled back, letting the observant policewoman in her take over as she studied the four on stage.

At a guess, they were in their mid-thirties, though if she hadn't seen Daniel closer at hand she'd have thought him younger, with his plentiful blond hair and blue eyes. Adam, the man who was speaking, was thin and dark-haired with narrow shoulders and an air of intense, almost desperate, sincerity.

But it was the women whom Nina found most interesting. Sarah, who had greeted them, was listening intently to her colleague, and in repose her face was sterner and less attractive, her pallor—which Nina hadn't previously noted—accentuated by a total lack of make-up. She was wearing a grey wool dress, the plainness of which was relieved only by the ornate Celtic cross hanging round her neck. Something in her stillness and total concentration hinted at an iron will and rigid self-discipline. Nina found it slightly chilling.

The other woman—Mattie, was it?—was even more daunting. Small where Sarah was tall, she was wearing an unbecoming jumper which was obviously hand-knitted and a lopsided skirt that seemed too big for her. Her eyes were deep-set and fixed unblinkingly on the back of Adam's head as he continued his address, and she'd an exceptionally high forehead on to which her mousy hair grew in a pronounced widow's peak. That was its only licence, the rest of it being scraped severely back and fastened at the nape of her neck.

An interesting and unusual quartet, Nina decided, wondering what their positions were in the hierarchy. Adam's introductory speech had been slick and professional, with a touch of humour to put people at their ease. Now, having warmed up his audience, he embarked at last on the main purpose of the gathering.

'Now, although I've told you our names, I haven't introduced us properly, because the important thing is that we belong to the Church of the Final Revelation.' He smiled. 'Yes, I know—another of these strange cults! It's true that over the last few decades many different movements have come into being. It's something that always happens at the end of a century, when people are fearful of what the future holds. The late eighteen-hundreds saw the rise of Spiritism, Christian Science, Theosophy and many others. Now we have the Moonies, Scientology, Hare Krishna and so on, all seeking a way through the maze.

'The difference is that this time, my friends, we do right to fear the future. During this last century man has caused more destruction than in any other since the world began, laying waste huge stretches of the planet, polluting its

atmosphere and slaughtering its creatures for profit. Now
the price must be paid, which is what makes our work so
urgent.'

Adam paused, his glittering eyes raking the rows of faces
upturned towards him. No one moved; there was total
silence. Confident of their attention, he drew a deep breath
and continued.

'Our Movement was born, like many others, in the
United States, at the divine inspiration of Captain Noah
Bellringer. Now, though still relatively new in this country,
it's one of the fastest growing groups in the world, and I
feel I can do no better than let our founder himself tell you
about it.'

On cue, the screen behind him was suddenly illuminated
and as he signalled to the girl at the light switch, the room
dimmed. Here we go, Nina thought. Let's see what they
come up with.

The hum of the projector started and a man's face filled
the screen. Although it was strongly formed—hooked nose,
deep-set eyes under bushy brows, a thatch of grey hair—
the overriding impression was of compassion. In fact, Nina
realized, it was disconcertingly like her childhood image of
God—a kindly old gentleman who peered down from the
sky.

As he began to speak, she concentrated on being professionally impartial. It wasn't easy. His voice had a soothing, hypnotic quality and he spoke slowly in a soft American
accent, seeming to address each one of them individually.

On the face of it, the message was one she'd heard before:
man's wanton disobedience, the despoiling of the planet,
the approach of doom. Yet she found herself at some basic
level responding to his urgency, moved—even alarmed—
by the threat of imminent catastrophe which he alone could
overcome, and his powerful plea to them to join him.

'And just what is this salvation I'm offering?' he asked.
'Be patient, my friends, for it is too overwhelming to be
revealed all at one time. We must prepare you gradually,
as the Lord prepared me before he revealed his purpose.'

A disappointed ripple went round the room, with which Nina sympathized. They were not, after all, to be handed salvation on a plate.

'I accept,' Bellringer was continuing, 'that some of you might not wish to go further. Perhaps you choose not to believe our message, or, even if you do, prefer to bury your heads and ignore it. So be it. But those of you who want to build a future for yourselves and your children, you, I am confident, will come back again and again. And it is to you that, over the coming weeks, we shall pass on our torch of knowledge.'

The slow, measured voice stopped. For a moment longer the face, trustworthy, reassuring, remained on the screen. Then it was gone, and they were left blinking in the brightness as the lights came on again.

Nina shook herself, aware that she'd been held more deeply than she'd intended by that mesmeric voice. Beside her, Pam whispered, 'What a wonderful man!'

She nodded. On the dais Adam rose to his feet again.

'Ladies and gentlemen, I hope you'll want to continue with us along the path to salvation. The next meeting, at the same time on Wednesday, will be much less formal. We'll split into groups so we can get to know each other and you'll start to learn something of our amazing plans for survival. Don't worry about committing yourself; you can withdraw from the programme at any stage you wish. In the meantime, there are some leaflets giving the background to our Movement which will help you prepare for the meeting, so do please take one as you leave.

'Now'—he smiled down on his audience—'we can all relax. There's coffee and biscuits at the end of the room, but to close the formal part of the evening I'll just say thank you for coming, good night, and God bless you.'

The other three on the dais had risen while he was speaking, and as he finished they all stepped down, separating and mingling with the audience. Nina stood up and looked about her. Most people were still in their seats, dazed-looking and seeming unwilling to move, but a few were making their way towards the table where coffee was being dispensed. As a gradual hum of conversation built up, she caught the words 'charismatic', 'inspiring', 'incredible'. A few rows behind her the two girls she'd noticed earlier were sitting close together, not speaking. They looked shell-shocked. She wondered again if their mothers knew they were here. The dark one, with her frizzy hair and straight brows, reminded her uncannily of her younger self.

Pam was saying, 'Will you come back on Wednesday?'

Nina hesitated. 'If I can,' she hedged.

'Me too. I feel so much better than when I arrived. More hopeful, somehow. I think it's knowing everyone here is my friend.'

'Yes,' Nina said inadequately. She smiled and nodded as Pam moved away, glancing back at the girls. She'd go and have a word with them, she decided, try to deflect any undue influence they might have been subjected to.

But people were at last stirring themselves, emerging from their rows and jamming the central aisle in front of her. Before she could reach the girls, two young men who had earlier been handing round drinks slid into the row in front of them and, leaning over the chair-backs, engaged them in conversation.

Damn! Nina thought—just what she'd wanted to forestall. As she drew level one of the boys said something, making them laugh, and, since there was no way she could approach them, she continued her slow progress down the aisle.

As they emerged from it, everyone else turned towards the coffee table where there was now quite a crowd, and she approached the door alone. Daniel, standing there with a handful of leaflets, raised his eyebrows at her.

'Not staying for coffee, Nina?'

So, despite the dozens of people he'd met, he'd re-membered her name. More salesmanship, but again she was warmed by it.

'I have to go,' she said awkwardly.

'You'll be back on Wednesday, won't you?'

She smiled noncommittally, took the leaflet he handed her and went out into the cool October night. The skies were clear and scattered with stars. She stood for a moment at the top of the steps, gazing upwards. Just what had happened in there this evening? That something had, she was in no doubt. Perhaps the recorder in her handbag would pinpoint it.

Love, she thought as she walked quickly to the corner and turned towards home. *Love, trust, salvation.* She frowned, trying to recall the words of Noah Bellringer and of Adam who had introduced him. But all that came to her was *love, trust, salvation*, and the phrase repeated itself like a litany all the way home.

When Nina turned into the gateway her mother was at the window, holding the curtain aside as she peered out. Nina waved, the curtain dropped back into place, and the front door opened as she reached it.

'How did it go?' Mrs Paxton demanded anxiously, before her daughter was properly in the house. 'Was it the people you thought? I've been that worried I've not been able to settle all evening.'

'Sorry, Mum, but as you see, I'm still in one piece.' Nina hung her anorak on the hook. 'Yes, it was them all right. And it was weird, there's no denying it. I recorded the speeches—would you like to hear them?'

'I most certainly would. You go through, and I'll bring the cocoa.'

The little front room was cosy with the fire glowing, the lamp on, and the television flickering silently in the corner. Mrs Paxton came in with the tray and set it on the low table by the fire.

'I'm ready for this,' Nina commented, picking up her mug. 'You'll be glad to hear I didn't drink anything while I was there, though I had difficulty making them take no for an answer.'

Her mother's eyes widened. 'You're never saying there was something in the drinks?'

'I don't know,' Nina said slowly. 'I thought I was just being paranoid, but now I'm not so sure. There could have been some kind of relaxant, to make us more receptive. Quite a few of them looked a bit woozy by the end of the evening.'

Beneath her mother's concerned exclamation, the words *love, trust, salvation* still lingered in her mind, though less stridently now she was back in familiar surroundings.

'Anyway,' she said firmly, setting down her mug, 'see what you think.' She switched on the recorder, and they sat in silence through Adam's opening speech. Then, as the gentle American voice filled the room, Nina tensed, waiting for the sense of oneness she had experienced in that crowded room.

It did not come. The words that had stirred her before now sounded hollow and empty, mere rhetoric. She was filled with a sense of betrayal, not helped by her mother's reaction as the recording ended.

'Well, what's so special about that, I'd like to know? All that about spoiling the planet—it's what we hear every day. And why get everyone there, build up their expectations, and then not even tell them what he was on about? A con, that's what I call it. If it had been me, I'd have walked out.'

Nina smiled painfully, doubting that. Had she been there, her mother would have been as spellbound as everyone else, but it was useless trying to explain.

And she'd been right—neither Adam nor Bellringer had used the actual words that had haunted her. So where had they come from? Had there been a subliminal message flashing on the screen, something so swift only the subconscious could register it? Was that what had held them in thrall?

She shuddered involuntarily. It had all seemed so innocuous, and yet . . .

She'd have a word with the DCI on Monday, she decided. In the meantime she'd try to put it out of her mind and enjoy her weekend.

*

Mattie Hendrix skirted a crowd of drunks on the corner of Gloucester Circus and turned into Station Road. Farther along, it degenerated into one of Shillingham's least desirable areas, some of the town's meanest streets lying behind its eastern frontage.

Thankfully, Mattie lived only a short way from the Circus and on the west side of the road, in a one-room flat above the Co-op. It was a good twenty minutes' walk from the school, slightly less from Victoria Drive. There were buses, of course, but she took them only if it was raining or she happened to be late. Every penny must be saved towards her future—her future, and that of the world.

She turned the key in her front door, letting herself into the tiny linoleum-floored hallway at the bottom of the steep staircase. It had been a shock to see the girls there tonight—she still wasn't sure how to tackle it. She knew she was expected to spread the word among the pupils at Ashbourne, but that was yet another area in which she had failed. Her faith was deep and vital to her, but she was no evangelist and that was a lack in her.

The stairs ended in the one-room flat. Mattie went to draw the thin curtains, glancing longingly at the black bars of the electric fire. Perhaps if she lit it for just ten minutes, to take the chill off the room, that wouldn't be too extravagant.

She switched it on and made herself a cup of tea in the curtained alcove she thought of as the kitchen. It had been a good turn-out tonight and Adam had done well. She knew he dreaded the evenings he was in charge.

Should she mention the meeting when she saw the girls on Monday? Would they tell their friends about seeing her there? Not, of course, that it was anything shameful, but the Captain had warned them of the hostility they must expect when they spoke of their beliefs. As he pointed out, Satan was always ready to mock and revile those who served the Lord.

She removed her coat with a shiver, noticing as she did so that another hole had appeared in her jumper. Something else that must be attended to before she went to bed.

She sat down with her tea at the rickety table and removed a bulky mass of exercise books from her satchel. With these essays to mark, she wouldn't have time for her gospel tonight—it was nearly eleven already. She'd have to set the alarm an hour early and work on it in the morning.

But what, she agonized, should she do about the girls?

When Hannah had gone and the front door was duly locked and bolted, Dilys stood for a moment, feeling the house fold itself peaceably about her. There was silence except for the soft shifting of the sitting-room fire as it subsided into ash.

Hannah was right, she thought, Hassocks was full of character—well worn and comfortable. As the old house settled for the night, Dilys walked slowly up the stairs, her thoughts returning to the guests who would shortly be thrust upon her.

Two spare bedrooms led off the L-shaped landing, each with its own bathroom, and on impulse she opened the door of the larger one where, presumably, the nanny would sleep.

She gave it a swift mental check. Tissues on the dressing-table, clock radio by the bed, plenty of hangers in the wardrobe. This time next week, a stranger would be sleeping here. What would she be like?

Suddenly, unaccountably, Dilys shivered, and as she retreated to the landing, remembered her mother's macabre phrase, 'Someone walked over my grave.'

For heaven's sake, she thought as she reached her own room. She'd be reading the teacups next! Her trouble, as she'd admitted to Hannah, was that she was altogether too self-absorbed. Well, one way or another, the next three weeks should shake her up a bit. With which glum reflection she began to prepare for bed.

CHAPTER 3

She was going to be late, Christina thought anxiously, easing the car out of the Heathrow sliproad on to the M4. The shuttle flight had been delayed and it had taken longer than usual to get out of the long-term car park. Which meant she wouldn't have time to call at the office before her lunch appointment.

Stephie would be back at school now; too bad this trip had coincided with her *exeat*, but it wasn't every day one had the chance to meet the head of an American hotel chain—one who, moreover, though in the UK only for the weekend, had specifically requested a meeting. And it seemed to have gone well; she must put Belinda straight on to working out the quotations. If they could get in with Bryant Hotels, she thought jubilantly, they would be made.

Her lunch appointment could also be fruitful. She'd not yet met Mr Derringer, who lived in the south of the county. He was staying at the King's Head for a few days on business, which was where they were meeting. The hotel had just reopened after a year's closure for refurbishment, which, according to the *Broadshire News*, had incorporated more *en suite* facilities and a leisure complex in the basement. A pity she couldn't have landed *that* contract, Christina thought ruefully. Still, it would be interesting to see what they'd made of it.

And here at last was the Shillingham junction. She turned thankfully off the motorway and twenty minutes later was in the hotel car park.

As soon as she pushed her way through the swing doors she was disorientated. Gone was the solid, old-fashioned ambience which had been the hotel's hallmark, the heavy chairs and thick velvet curtains. Instead, there were pale wood panels, glass doors showing a transformed lounge, and an overall luminescence far removed from the pervading gloom she was used to.

The chief surprise, though, was that on this Monday lunch-time the foyer was thronged with people. How, she thought despairingly, was she going to find her client in this crowd? 'In the bar,' she'd suggested unthinkingly. Now, she wasn't even sure where it was.

Fighting her way through the throng, she was grateful to see arrows indicating the direction of bar and restaurant, and a board at the foot of the stairs explained at least part of the activity: two separate conferences were in progress, and no doubt both had disgorged their delegates for the lunch break.

The bar, too, had metamorphosed, shedding its twenties-style chrome and glass-topped tables for an opulence of rich wood, deep sofas, and waist-high fretted divisions offering an illusion of privacy. On a stand in the middle of the room was a magnificent bronze of a horse: Copper Coin, no doubt, the chestnut which had won the Broadminster Cup for three successive seasons.

The professional part of Christina longed to study the décor in detail; ideas could be gleaned from an imaginative overhaul like this. Unfortunately, though, it would have to wait, and she raked the room for a man alone, one who was no doubt by this time becoming restive.

At once she spotted a likely candidate, seated in one of the low-backed alcoves. There was a briefcase at his feet, and even as she registered him, he glanced with obvious impatience at his watch. In fact, she thought apprehensively, everything about him indicated that he was on edge, from his frequent glances towards the door to the staccato tapping of his cigarette against the glass ashtray in front of him. She'd obviously have to turn on maximum charm to make up for her lateness.

Making her way towards him, she saw that he was younger than she'd imagined from their phone calls—rather attractive, in fact, if he'd only relax—with dark springing hair and a slight cleft in his chin.

'Mr Derringer?' she said, holding out her hand.

He looked up in surprise, then rose, taking her hand as he returned her smile. 'Unfortunately, no!' he said.

'Oh!' Christina stared at him, momentarily nonplussed. 'I do beg your pardon. I'm meeting someone I don't know, and I assumed—'

'Please don't worry—it's my pleasure. I'm expecting someone too. Why don't you join me and we can wait together? Can I get you a drink?'

'Oh no, really, I must look for—'

'Nonsense. I need another anyway. What'll it be?'

But no sooner had he reached the bar than a voice behind her said hesitantly, 'Mrs French? I thought I overheard— I'm Robert Derringer.'

She felt a spurt of disappointment, accepting that lunch with the man she'd approached would have been more enjoyable. Derringer was in his fifties, bald, bespectacled, and—a frequent occurrence—several inches shorter than herself. Still, it was a business rather than social engagement and he could put a very worthwhile contract in her hands if she landed him successfully.

Having made her apologies to the other man—fortunately before he'd paid for her drink—she set herself to do so. It was some ten minutes later that, from the corner of her eye, she saw him leaving the room with a man and woman. By the time she and Derringer reached the restaurant, she'd forgotten all about him.

Detective Chief Inspector David Webb added seasoning to the pan on the stove, stirred it, and tasted the contents. Satisfied, he turned from the cooker, glanced at Hannah who was perched on the kitchen table, and said without preamble, 'Ever heard of the Revvies?'

She raised her eyebrows. 'As in motorbikes?'

He grinned. 'No, as in members of the Church of the Final Revelation.'

'Good heavens! No, I haven't.'

'That's the colloquial name, I'm told.'

'Less of a mouthful, certainly. Whoever are they?'

'One of these new religious movements. An American import, but expanding rapidly over here.'

Hannah sipped her gin and tonic. 'And what's your interest in them?'

'My WDI came to see me this morning. She went to one of their meetings to suss them out and wasn't very happy with her findings.'

'In what way?'

'She suspects the pre-meeting coffee was spiked—though as she didn't have any that's pure speculation. And she's pretty sure the film they were shown was subliminally doctored.'

'How very sinister.'

Webb filled a large pan with water, salted it, and set it to boil. 'Yes, not a pleasant thought.'

'What actually happened?'

'It was just a warm-up session, whetting the appetite and hinting at marvels to come. They wouldn't want to lay their goods on the line till they're sure they've hooked their audience.'

'But you think they could be dangerous?'

'All cults are dangerous, Hannah. Some are benevolent and some not, but they're all out to get you. For your own good, of course, as they go to some lengths to explain. Trouble is, it's often the weak and vulnerable who are attracted to them, and fall straight into their clutches without realizing it.'

The water rose up the pan and he tipped a measured quantity of spaghetti into it. Hannah slid to the floor and prepared to lay the table.

'Did I tell you I saw Dilys last week?' she asked, opening the cutlery drawer.

'No, how is she?'

'Up to ninety, poor love. She's being invaded by her god-daughter's baby, plus nanny. They'll be there for three weeks, and she's dreading every minute of it.'

'Can't say I blame her. How's the writer's block?'

'Still with her, and this is hardly the remedy.'

Webb made sympathetic noises. He'd never met Dilys, but since Hannah often spoke of her, felt he knew her quite well. Like Hannah's other friends, she was unaware of his existence; deputy headmistresses, especially those of prestigious private schools, could ill afford gossip, and Hannah had decided right at the beginning that it was wiser to keep her own counsel where affairs of the heart were concerned.

Picking up the bottle of Chianti, he followed her through to the living-room. It looked its best at this time of day, he thought contentedly, the lamps lit and—since he'd not yet turned on the heating—the glow of the gas fire to dispel the evening chill.

When he first came here, soon after his divorce, the flat had been simply somewhere to sleep and keep his belongings. But gradually he'd stamped his personality on the place and it had evolved from an impersonal set of rooms into a home.

He stood in the doorway, taking unaccustomed stock and approving what he saw: white paintwork and pale cinnamon walls on which were displayed the carefully chosen paintings which accounted for most of his spare cash; the oak dining-table he'd picked up for a song before antiques became big business; deep, welcoming armchairs, each with its small table alongside to accommodate glass or papers; a glass-fronted bookcase; his desk, and, in the corner, his easel and the pile of canvases stacked against the wall.

Conscious of how much he learned about people from their surroundings, he wondered for the first time what his own home said about him.

Hannah's voice recalled him from his musings. 'Any chance of opening that bottle, or are you going to stand there holding it all evening?'

He grinned apologetically, moved into the room and set it on the table.

She bent to read the label. 'Which glasses shall we use?'

'Oh, just the everyday ones. I'll—'

'It's all right, I know where they are.'

Still retrospective, he walked to the window and stood, as he did most evenings, staring down the hill towards the lights of Shillingham.

Though his flat wasn't as spacious as Hannah's on the floor below, there were definite advantages to being at the top of the building. It was like a watchtower, with the town spread out below for his inspection. And somewhere among those lights, he thought suddenly, as today's concerns reasserted themselves, it was possible that a new menace was moving.

Hannah, returning with the glasses, glanced across at him. 'You *are* pensive this evening,' she remarked. 'Still brooding about the Revvies?'

'I don't like manipulation,' he said shortly, 'which is what it all boils down to.'

'But who are these people? What's their message?'

He felt in his pocket and extracted the crumpled publicity sheet Nina had given him. 'Does this logo suggest anything to you?'

She moved to take it from him, studying the triangle with the curved line above it. 'Not really.'

'Suppose that arc was coloured.' He paused. 'Multi-coloured.'

'A rainbow?'

'Right. And the other shape?'

'A triangle?' He shook his head. She studied it further. 'I suppose it could be a simplified drawing of a mountain.'

'Ten out of ten! A mountain and a rainbow. Now—any bright ideas?'

'Noah?' she hazarded facetiously.

'Noah indeed!'

Her eyes widened. 'You're not serious?'

'Oh, but I am. Their theory is that another Flood's on the way, and they'll be the only ones to survive it.'

'They're not building an ark?' Hannah's voice was incredulous.

'Not exactly.' A smile lifted his mouth. 'Incidentally,

their founder's name is Bellringer. Would you believe *Noah* Bellringer?'

Hannah gazed at him. 'Now you really are joking.'

'Without a word of a lie. Born and raised, as they say, in the Bible Belt of America.'

'But—the Flood? Noah and the *Flood?* He changed his name to fit the theory?'

'No, it's been verified on his birth certificate. Mind you, the association of ideas must have played its part.'

'But if they're not building an ark, what do they intend to do?'

Webb moved to the table and poured Chianti into the glasses. 'I'm told they're investing heavily in high ground— the more mountainous the better. They already have settlements in Scotland, Wales and the Lake District.'

'They're taking it pretty seriously, then. When is this Flood due? Should I be keeping an eye on the weather forecast?'

'Don't hold your breath. It's one of the many joys promised for the millennium. Right'—he took the paper back and stuffed it into his pocket—'enough of all this nonsense. The spaghetti should be ready, so let's eat.'

Daniel Stacey eased the car through the gateway of No. 5, Victoria Drive and parked on the concrete base which had replaced the front garden. He was bone-tired, but it would be hours yet before he was free to go to bed. Adam's space was still empty, though Lucy's ancient Morris stood in its accustomed corner. It was Lucy's week as cook, he remembered, and hoped she'd kept something hot for him.

He eased himself out of the car, locked it, and stretched, rubbing his aching back. Then he walked briskly up the steps and let himself into the house. Immediately he was conscious of warmth and comfort and his tiredness began to drop away. In thirty-five years, this was the only place he'd felt at home.

At the end of the passage the kitchen door opened and

Lucy peered out at him. 'Ah, there you are! I was beginning to think you'd got lost.'

He went towards her, relishing the savoury smell which came to meet him. 'It's my week to oversee prep, I forgot to tell you. Have the others eaten?'

'All except Adam, he's not back yet. Are you ready for yours?'

'More than ready—I'm starving.' He walked past her into the warm, bright kitchen and washed his hands at the sink. Lucy took a casserole from the oven, dished out a generous portion, and put the plate on the long scrubbed table.

'Roll on half-term!' Daniel said, seating himself in front of it. He was a PE master at Shillingham Grammar School and grateful that as such he was spared the preparation and marking which continually hung over poor Mattie, making it almost impossible to concentrate on her gospel. Apart from taking his turn on the prep rota, his evenings were his own.

He bowed his head, said a silent Grace, and began to eat. Lucy slid into the seat opposite with a mug of coffee.

'Hard day?'

'Much the same as usual. I did some canvassing in the lunch hour, which was a bit of a rush. This is great, Luce.'

'Good. Did you have any luck?'

He paused, thinking back to the calls he'd made. 'Hard to tell. I didn't do badly on collecting, but whether any of them will show up on Wednesday is anyone's guess.'

'Think any of the Friday lot will?'

'I hope so.' More particularly he hoped Nina would, but pushed the thought aside. He'd been disconcerted to find how often over the weekend she'd come into his mind.

'Vince thinks those two schoolgirls will be back. They seemed quite keen to know more.'

Daniel smiled tiredly. 'Or perhaps just to see him again. But whatever the reason, the oftener they come, the more chance we have of saving them. Which, after all, is what counts.'

'Amen,' Lucy said automatically.

He glanced at her with affection. She was a plump, pleasant-faced girl, always ready to help out and take on extra work if need be. She and Liz were the only two in the house who were unemployed, and he knew it worried them. The Captain actively encouraged his flock to be self-supporting, though Daniel sometimes wondered if he appreciated the strain of a full-time job in addition to the amount of work they were required to do for the Church. Adam would even now be canvassing his way round Shillingham, after being on his feet all day in the shop he managed.

Daniel pushed his plate away and looked at his watch. Eight-thirty. Time for an hour's work before evening prayers.

'Thanks for the meal, Lucy. See you.'

'See you,' she echoed, watching him leave the room. Down the hall the front door opened and closed and the sound of voices reached her. Adam was back. She stood up and went once more to the oven.

Adam had looked exhausted, Daniel thought as he entered his room, but Monday was always a late night. After prayers the household meeting was held, with discussions on fund-raising, housekeeping and accounts, and any problems that might have arisen during the week. There were eight of them resident in the house, and by the time each had made his or her report it was usually past midnight. At least the pressure on finances had been eased by what promised to be a handsome legacy. Thank God for it, he thought devoutly. The Captain always said if they had faith enough, the funds would be provided.

He drew the curtains and sat down at his desk, pulling his files towards him. As he did so, his eyes fell on his grandmother's photograph in its silver frame, and he felt a stab of guilt. It was time he wrote to her; the least he could do, after—he smiled wryly—all she'd done for him. It was a phrase which had echoed through his childhood, as though it was his fault he'd been illegitimate.

Liz was, too, he remembered. She'd mentioned it casually once, surprising him by her unconcern. But hers had been a large, lower middle-class family with plenty of love to go round, and the lack of a father here and there was of little consequence.

He lifted the photograph, staring into the strong, lined face that gazed back at him. Though kind enough in her way, she was an undemonstrative woman and it had never occurred to her that he was starved of love. Small wonder he'd felt so isolated. Until he discovered the Church.

He smiled fleetingly, putting the photograph down again. *His* church, that is. The standard one had been an integral part of his upbringing, but his childhood God was a remote and awesome figure Who, though he'd been taught to address Him as 'Father', had remained as distant, mysterious and unreal as his own father had been. Thank God— quite literally thank God—he'd been rescued by the Revelationists.

Abandoning his memories, Daniel opened the file and settled down to work.

Christina stretched luxuriously, and Edward, watching her, smiled. 'If this was a film, one of us would reach for a cigarette!'

'Not these days, surely.'

'I don't know that anyone's come up with a substitute. Anyway, my love, you'll gather that I'm more than pleased to have you home again.'

'Me too. But apart from missing me, how was the weekend?'

'Oh, the competition was a great success—record number of entries, and the weather stayed fine.'

'I meant with Stephanie,' she said, reproach in her voice.

'Oh. Well, she was OK. Not that I saw much of her, actually; she was off with Marina most of the time, and, of course, I was at the club. One odd thing, though. She announced that she'd gone vegetarian.'

'What?' Christina turned her head on the pillow to stare at him.

'Really. Just suddenly came out with it. Wanted a note to take back to school.'

'Saying what, for heaven's sake?'

'Asking that her wishes be respected.'

'Good Lord. When did this come up?'

'Just after you'd gone on Saturday morning, when I asked if she fancied some bacon and eggs.'

'Well, if she keeps it up in the holidays she'll have to make do with whatever vegetables we're having. I've better things to do than plan alternative menus for her ladyship.'

He said slowly, 'There was something else odd, too. When she'd gone back to school I went into her room to retrieve the sweater she'd borrowed, and I saw she'd tipped all her make-up and scent into the wastepaper basket.'

'Oh love, that can't be right. She spends most of her allowance on make-up, she wouldn't throw it away.'

'Go and see for yourself. And there was that bottle of scent she begged and begged for, for her birthday. Cost me an arm and a leg, I seem to remember, and there it was, only half-used, in the bin.'

'Then I shall retrieve it myself,' Christina said decidedly. 'Whatever's got into the child?'

'Some passing fad, no doubt. Now, what about your trip? You haven't told me any details; was it worthwhile?'

'Oh, I think so. Belinda's been working out figures all afternoon. If we can get in with Bryant Hotels we'll be in the big time.'

Her thoughts moved on. 'And as soon as I got back I had that lunch appointment at the King's Head. Have you been since it reopened? It's very plush now—all different shades of wood and lamps everywhere.' She gave a little laugh. 'And you'll be interested to hear I tried to pick someone up!'

'I *beg* your pardon?'

'Really. Rather a dishy man, actually. I saw him sitting alone frowning at his watch and was sure he was my lunch

date, so I went over to him. But as soon as we'd sorted
ourselves out and he'd offered me a drink, the real Mr
Derringer arrived, and that was that.'

'And was the real Mr Derringer "dishy" too?'

'Far from it. But much more importantly, he's on the
point of signing a contract.'

'Good for him. And what happened to your deserted
swain?'

'Oh, his friends turned up eventually—I saw him leave
with them. I bet they had a laugh about the blonde who
tried to get off with him!'

But the handsome stranger wasn't laughing now. He was
at that moment lolling in an armchair in his darkened room
at the King's Head. And he was dead.

CHAPTER 4

Dilys watched the car turn into the drive, arranged a smile
on her face and went to open the door. The rhus in the
border, she noticed, had started to redden—proof, if proof
were needed, of the relentless march of time towards the
date when her manuscript must be delivered. And now this.

'This' was in the process of emerging from the car, held
tightly in his mother's arms. Sebastian was a placid baby,
secure in the love that surrounded him and confident of
getting his own way. Dilys returned his stare somewhat
doubtfully.

'Darling!' Susie planted an enthusiastic kiss on her cheek.
'You're an angel! I've stressed to Sarah that you mustn't
be disturbed in any way.'

Dilys's eyes moved to the young woman who was helping
James extract a folding cot from the boot. 'One point,
Susie,' she said quickly, remembering Peggy's reservations.
'Where does she sit in the evenings? I mean—'

'Oh, don't worry about that. If it's convenient, she goes

out. Seb never wakes once he's put down, so provided
there's someone in the house we don't mind. She has relatives in the town and spends most of her free time with
them. And if she's in, she works in her room.'

Dilys was relieved that neither she nor Peggy would be
called on to entertain their visitor. 'Works?' she repeated
with a raised eyebrow.

'For some exam or other,' Susie said vaguely. 'She keeps
very much to herself. She has breakfast and lunch with Seb
and supper on a tray in her room. Honestly, you'll hardly
know she's here.'

James and Sarah approached them with what seemed an
inordinate amount of baggage. James bent to kiss Dilys's
cheek, and Susie continued:

'Dilly, this is Sarah Baines. Miss Hayward, Sarah.'

Dilys smiled and nodded, disconcerted to find the young
woman's gaze as uncommunicative as Sebastian's. However, she smiled gravely and the moment was eased by
James's inquiry as to where the luggage should be taken.

'I'll lead the way.' Dilys turned back to the house and
went up the stairs with the contingent following behind her.

'This is Miss Baines's room,' she announced, aware of
sounding formal but unable for some reason to call the stiff
young woman by her first name. And unbidden, the
memory returned of her involuntary shiver the previous
week when checking the room for her guest.

She moved hastily down the landing. 'And this is Sebastian's,' she continued. 'There isn't a general bathroom—
each room has its own. The next door is the little room
where we do the ironing—the airing cupboard's in there—
and the one at the end is my room. If there's anything you
need,' she added to Sarah, 'do please ask either me or my
housekeeper.'

'Thank you, I'm sure everything will be fine.'

James went into the baby's room and began to set up
the cot, while Sarah, depositing various bundles on the bed,
unrolled the mattress. Susie turned to her son. 'Now, my
darling, you're going to be a good boy for Auntie Dilly,

aren't you? And Mummy and Daddy will be back before you know it.'

Sudden tears filled her eyes and she hid them by burying her face in the baby's neck and kissing him.

'Have you time for coffee?' Dilys asked, to distract her.

'No thank you, we must be going. The car's coming for us at eleven. Now don't worry,' she added, intercepting Dilys's cautious glance at the baby. 'Sarah's very experienced—she'll take good care of him.'

'I'm sure she will,' Dilys said, unsure whether it was herself or the baby's mother she was reassuring. James and Sarah emerged from the bedroom, where the cot now stood in the centre of the floor.

'We'd better be going, darling.'

'I know.'

Susie thrust her son into Sarah's arms and turned blindly to the stairs. James, with a wry little smile, said goodbye to the nanny and followed Dilys downstairs. Moments later the car had driven away.

Dilys went through to the kitchen, where Peggy had been keeping a low profile. 'All right, Peggy, you can relax. She either goes out in the evenings or spends them in her room.'

'Well, that's a relief.' The woman paused. 'What's she like?'

'Not what I'd expected.' She'd imagined a fresh-faced girl with a ready smile. 'In her mid-thirties, I'd say, and rather severe-looking. Still, if she's as devoted and efficient as Susie says, that's all that matters.'

So the invasion had taken place. Dilys devoutly hoped it would have no inhibiting effect on her thought processes.

'I'm going to the study,' she said.

'Ken?'

Sergeant Jackson straightened in his chair. 'Yes, Guv?'

'That sudden death at the King's Head: Pringle's not happy with it. I'll meet you at the gate in five minutes. No point in taking the car.'

'Right, Guv.'

Jackson dropped the phone back on its stand and glanced out of the window. The sun was shining—a great day to be out of the office, even if it meant dealing with some poor stiff at the King's Head.

He was whistling as he strolled past the pond in the station forecourt. It was Vicky's birthday at the end of the week—unbelievable to think she'd be eight. She'd set her heart on a video game, Millie said, but there was no way she was getting one. Jackson didn't hold with them on various counts, not the least being cost. In any case he'd rather she played outdoors like kids always used to, instead of being cooped up all day in front of the telly.

Quick footsteps behind him announced Webb's arrival, and Jackson prepared to adjust his shorter stride to his chief's long lope as they set off down Carrington Street.

'So what have we got, Guv?'

'The chambermaid found him when she went to do the bed. In his chair, apparently without a mark on him, but Pringle smells a rat, not least because they don't know who he is. No identification at all: money in his wallet, but no credit cards, cheque-book, driving licence or diary and no clues in his overnight bag.'

'He must have registered, surely?'

'I'd have thought so. We'll sort it out when we get there.'

They had turned the corner into the busier thoroughfare of Duke Street and had to raise their voices to be heard over the heavy traffic.

'And there's no obvious cause of death?' Jackson asked.

'Seems not, but I'd back Pringle's suspicions any day.'

They walked on in silence until they reached Gloucester Circus, the busy centre of the town where, like spokes from a wheel, no fewer than five main roads radiated in all directions. Waiting for the lights to change, Webb eyed the hotel directly opposite them. It had been a landmark of the town for as long as he could remember, but had been closed for a year or so while major refurbishment took place. No different from the outside anyway; probably a preservation order on it, he reflected.

The lights changed and they crossed to the other side and pushed their way through the swing doors.

'Fair smartened the old place up, haven't they?' Jackson commented, noting with approval the pale wood panelling and thick carpet. 'Don't think they'd welcome us for a pie and a pint these days, Guv!'

'It was never my scene,' Webb returned shortly. He approached the reception desk. 'DCI Webb, Shillingham CID.'

'Yes, sir, Mr Diccon is expecting you. He'll show you up, if you'd like to come this way.'

They were whisked smartly into an elaborately appointed office. A tall, thin man with over-long dark hair and a pale face rose from behind a desk.

'Ah, good morning, gentlemen. This is terrible—terrible. And coming so soon on our reopening, too.' He was almost wringing his hands.

'If you could take us straight up, sir,' Webb interposed smoothly, 'we'd be glad of a word later.'

'Yes, of course.' Diccon led them down a short corridor to what was obviously the service lift, no doubt to protect the sensibilities of the other guests.

'I understand there's some question about the deceased's identity?' Webb said, as they waited for it to arrive. 'Surely he checked in on arrival?'

'Alas, no,' Diccon replied. 'He arrived yesterday around lunch-time, our busiest period. We have two conferences in progress and as you can imagine, the staff were under considerable pressure.'

The lift arrived, and they stepped into it, Diccon pressing the button for the second floor. 'And as luck would have it,' he continued, 'what with lunch breaks and so on, for just those few crucial minutes there was only one receptionist on the desk, and she was run off her feet. She scribbled down his name—which unfortunately she now can't decipher— and he took the key and said he'd check in later.'

The lift had stopped and they got out. 'I shall want to see the receptionist and the note she made.'

'Yes, of course.'

They were led along another corridor to a door, outside which PC Joe Kenworthy stood impassively on guard. Webb nodded to him. 'Dr Pringle still here?'

'Yes, sir, he's waiting for you.'

Webb opened the door and went in, pushing it shut behind him. The bedroom was the standard layout. Immediately to the left was a fitted wardrobe, to the right a door leading presumably to the bathroom. Twin beds protruded from the right-hand wall, while a luggage rack, dressing-table and mini-bar took up that on the left. At the far end, beneath the windows, stood a table and two easy chairs, and slumped in one of them was an inert body. Beside it, looking out of the window with his hands in his pockets, was the spare figure of Dr Pringle. He turned as Webb came in.

'Ah, Dave. Thought you'd like a wee look at this joker. No obvious cause of death but it smells a mite fishy to me.'

Webb had great respect for Pringle's nose. He walked over and stood looking down at the body.

The deceased was—or had been—a good-looking man in his forties. He had plentiful curly hair, dark brown in colour, and straight dark brows. His suit was fairly light-weight and the cut, from what Webb could see of it, didn't look entirely English.

'No ID, I gather.'

'No, that's what aroused my suspicions in the first place.'

Webb surveyed the position of the body, comfortably relaxed in its chair. 'If it was natural causes, wouldn't he have tried to reach the phone?'

The doctor shrugged. 'If it was heart, he mightn't have had time. But I don't think it *was* natural causes, Dave. Don't ask me why; apart from the ID business—which could have an innocent explanation—there's nothing I can put my finger on. It's more a hunch than anything, but I'd lay money on our having a suspicious death on our hands.'

'That's good enough for me. We'll get on to the Coroner's Officer and Scenes of Crime.'

Pringle nodded, satisfied.

'Care to stick your neck out on approximate time of death?'

The doctor grinned. 'Better leave that to friend Stapleton. Personally, I'd say around twenty-four hours.' He picked up his black bag. 'OK if I go just now? I've a full surgery waiting.'

'Yes, of course. Many thanks, Alec.'

Alone with the dead man, Webb stood for several minutes trying to soak up such atmosphere as there was in that sterile room. He believed firmly that a corpse had a lot to tell an investigator, and valued a space of time alone with the victim, always hoping some mysterious osmosis might occur.

What emotions had been experienced here during the last twenty-four hours? Despair? Suicide was still a possibility, though again, no discernible means. Fear? And if so, of what? A sudden pain in the chest? Or, even more threatening, someone standing over him as Webb did now? He was directly in front of the window, as the murderer—if murderer there were—would also have been. But could anyone have seen him or her? Webb doubted it. No windows gave directly on this one, and anyone standing in the car park below would have to crane his head back in order to see him.

He turned again to the suit. The jacket seemed baggier than usual, the trousers narrower. The shoes especially, now that he looked at them, had a decidedly continental look to them, with their supple leather and fringed tongues. But if he *was* a foreigner, then his passport and flight tickets were also missing.

Webb turned his attention to the case on the luggage rack. It was open, but its owner had not had time to unpack; pyjamas, shaving gear and toiletries were still inside, together with a change of underwear. A label on one of the garments was in French, which seemed to back his hunch, but there was an English paperback stuffed down the side of the case.

Webb looked round for a briefcase. If the victim was a businessman, which seemed likely, he would surely have had something of the kind. But a quick search proved futile, a fact which could be significant.

There was a macintosh hanging in the wardrobe, but its pockets revealed only a soiled handkerchief and half a tube of Polo mints. The bathroom contained nothing personal. It seemed the man had simply come to his room, dumped his mac and his case—and then what? It had been lunchtime: perhaps he'd gone straight down to the bar or restaurant and met someone there—but by chance or design? Or had he arranged a meeting in his room? With a woman, perhaps? That thought opened further possibilities. In any event, it seemed likely he'd died within an hour or so of arriving at the hotel. In heaven's name, why?

Webb sighed and rejoined Jackson, who'd been chatting to Joe Kenworthy at the door. 'Right, Joe, I want the room sealing till Dr Stapleton and the SOCOs get here. Bleep me when they arrive—I'll be in the hotel.'

And, nodding to Jackson to accompany him, Webb strode down the corridor towards the lift.

The manager was nervously awaiting them in his office.

'Now, sir,' Webb said briskly, 'I've given orders that in their own interests no one is to leave or enter the hotel until further notice. And as a matter of urgency, I shall need names and addresses of everyone who was here during the relevant time yesterday, together with a note of anyone who has since left, especially if it was earlier than anticipated.'

The manager was gazing at him in horror. 'But Chief Inspector, I can't have my guests treated as though they were criminals! I—'

'Mr Diccon,' Webb interrupted forcefully, 'one of your guests is dead, and it is possible he did not die from natural causes.'

'You mean—someone might have *killed* him? Here?'

'It's possible,' Webb repeated, biting back the acid comment that murderers were no respecters of refurbished hotels and their reputations. 'Everyone, staff and guests, will have to be interviewed as soon as possible. Someone might have seen something suspicious.'

With a shrug of resignation, Diccon lifted his phone and gave the necessary orders. The support group would be here any minute, Webb thought, but they'd already wasted twenty-four hours. The murderer was probably long gone. In the meantime he resumed the interview.

'Now, sir, you say the deceased didn't register on arrival. But surely he'd confirmed his booking in writing?'

'He hadn't booked in advance,' Diccon said, making an obvious effort to control himself. 'Arrived on spec. As I told you, he did give his name, but the girl was doing half a dozen things at once and can't decipher her scrawl. A two-syllabled name beginning with K is the best she can come up with.'

'You have it here?'

'Yes, as you asked.' He pushed across the reservations book. On the page for the previous day, the entry against room 251 was indeed all but illegible. An initial K was the only recognizable character, though an upper loop halfway along could, Webb supposed, be a b, d, h, l or even another k. Not a lot of help.

'Any idea how he arrived? Car in the car park, for instance?'

Diccon shrugged helplessly. 'We've no way of knowing. The ambulance man said he had car keys—I called them first, of course, and they were trying to discover who he was. But short of going round all the cars—'

'Our plain-clothes officers will see to that.' Diccon opened his mouth to protest once more, but catching Webb's eye, thought better of it. 'And now,' Webb continued smoothly, 'I'd like to see the receptionist, please, and after that the young lady who found the deceased.'

'Certainly.'

The receptionist must have been standing by; almost as soon as Diccon put down his phone she tapped on the door. He introduced her to Webb—her name, Samantha, was inscribed on the badge she wore—then tactfully left the room.

She was tall and slim, wore her hair in a ponytail high on her head, and her make-up was immaculate. Looking at her, Webb found it hard to imagine her being flustered or writing anything illegible.

'Sit down, Miss—er—Samantha. I understand you allocated the room to the guest who died?'

'That's right.' She seated herself gracefully. 'I feel dreadful that I took so little notice of him, but as I think Mr Diccon explained, I'd been left to hold the fort and quite frankly, it was chaos. Queues of people were waiting at the desk and the phone was ringing non-stop. When he offered to check in later, I was only too grateful.'

'I want you to think carefully, because this could be important. Had he a foreign accent?'

She looked surprised. 'No, sir.'

'Can you be sure, when you were so busy? If—'

'I should certainly remember if he'd been foreign,' she said decidedly.

'Even if he spoke good English?' Webb persisted, remembering the paperback.

'I would at least have registered it. We're trained to speak to guests in their own language if at all possible. And though I can't remember his name, it was an English one. I'm sure of that.'

'Ah yes, his name. You've not had any more thoughts on that?'

'I've been racking my brains all morning, but it won't come back. I know it began with K, and I'm pretty sure it had two syllables, but though I've gone through every name I can think of, none of them seems right.'

'He couldn't have been connected with either of the conferences? A speaker who'd been delayed, for instance?'

'No, they all arrived the previous evening. They'd have told us if anyone else was expected.'

'Can you remember exactly what he said?'

She frowned, thinking back. 'I was on the phone, and

the caller had gone to check something so I'd a moment
free. I looked up and he was at the front of the queue. He
smiled and said, "I'd no idea you'd be so busy. I'd like a
room for tonight, if you have one going."' She smiled
slightly. 'An English idiom, wouldn't you say, sir?'

Cheeky monkey! thought Jackson.

'Go on.'

'Well, I pulled over the reservations book and 251 was
vacant so I took the key off the hook and asked his name.'
She paused and Webb waited, not wanting to banish any
elusive memory by prompting her. But she sighed and
shook her head. 'I'd just started to write it in when the
person on the phone came back and took up the conversation where we'd left off, and I had to switch back to what
we'd been discussing. The key was in my hand and he—
Mr K—leant forward and took it, mouthing, "I'll check in
later" and that was the last I saw of him.'

'Did you notice how much luggage he had?'

'Sorry—though he bent to pick something up as he
turned away.'

And that was all she could tell him. Webb had to admit
it was a concise account. A pity her normal efficiency had
been impaired at the crucial moment.

The chambermaid was a very different case. Pale and
red-eyed, she shivered constantly throughout the interview,
which at first roused Webb's pity and later his irritation.
She was small, with wispy fair hair, and in response to his
question, admitted that her name was Maggie.

'You didn't see this gentleman at all the previous
evening?' Webb asked her. She shook her head, clenching
her hands in her lap.

'Not even when you went to turn the bed down?'

'We don't do that now, sir,' she whispered. 'So as not to
disturb the guests.'

To save themselves the trouble, more like. 'But you knew
the room was occupied?'

'Yes, a twin-bedded, let as a single.'

'Had he ordered a newspaper or early-morning tea?'

'No, sir. That's why I didn't go in till going on ten, to make the bed, like.'

'And what was your first impression on entering the room?'

'The—the stuffiness, sir.' She put a hand over her mouth and Jackson hoped fervently she was not about to vomit. 'Then I saw the gentleman sitting by the window, and that neither of the beds had been used. So I said "Sorry!" and started to go out again, but he looked kind of queer, so I went a bit closer, and—and then I could see—'

She sat gazing piteously at Webb, tears streaming down her face.

'It's all right, Maggie, you're doing very well. Did you notice anything else—anything in the room out of place, for instance?'

'The other chair was pulled round, like, to face the one he was in,' she said hesitantly. 'And it looked like someone had been sitting on the end of the bed.'

Webb leant forward. 'Did it now? As though two people had been with him?'

'I—I suppose so, sir.'

'Any cups, glasses, cigarette stubs?'

She shook her head, wiping her cheek with her hand.

'Did you touch anything? Anything at all?'

She stared at him with frightened eyes. 'I—I might have straightened the bedspread, sir. Sort of automatic, like.'

Webb closed his eyes briefly, hoping the spontaneous gesture wouldn't scupper the SOCOs' chances of lifting vital fibres.

'Anything in the wastepaper basket?' Such as a passport, some plane tickets, a clutch of credit cards? It had been empty when he'd glanced into it.

'I didn't look,' she confessed miserably. Nor could he blame her.

'Did you go into the bathroom?'

'No, sir. Once I saw he was—dead, I just ran out calling for Mrs Anderson. She's in charge of our floor, sir.'

Another hazard loomed. 'And what did Mrs Anderson do?' he asked heavily.

'She came in and had a look for herself.'

'And did *she* touch anything?'

'No, and she said I mustn't neither. Then she phoned for Mr Diccon.'

'From the phone in the room?'

'No, the one in the housemaids' room.'

Thank heaven for Mrs Anderson. He could leave her interview to someone else.

'Right, Maggie, I don't think we have any more questions for you. Thank you for your help.'

She nodded and crept from the room, closing the door softly. Webb stretched and looked at his watch. 'You've been remarkably forbearing, Ken. Do you know it's almost two?'

Jackson grinned. 'My stomach could have told you, Guv.'

'Let's go along to the bar and challenge them on the pie-and-pint stakes. I need a word with the barman, anyway. He might have spotted our lad as one particular needle in his haystack.'

Fortunately, the barman was one of those who'd been on duty the previous day. The lunch-time rush was now over and, having heard all the excitement, he was more than ready to chat to the detectives.

'We're trying to discover what our chap did after arriving at the hotel,' Webb said, having first placed his order to placate Jackson. 'Since it was around one o'clock he could easily have come in here.'

The barman shrugged. 'Wish I could help, sir, but the place was going like a fair. One solitary gent—'

'We're hoping he might have met someone.'

'People were meeting each other all over the place. It's what they come here for.'

Webb took a long draught of his beer. 'Come to think of it, he might have met *two* people. Is that any help?'

'Not with the conference mob in at the time.' He paused.

'The only bloke I remember is one who *lost* someone rather than met them.'

'How do you mean?'

'Well, he ordered a malt whisky and went to sit down. Then a few minutes later he came back and ordered another, plus a gin and tonic. I was just about to get them, when a lady came up and tapped him on the shoulder and said sorry, her friend had arrived and she couldn't join him after all, so he cancelled the gin.'

'He didn't suggest to her they joined up?' Webb was thinking of the two visitors upstairs.

'No, just said not to worry, the people he was expecting would be here soon.'

'People? In the plural?'

'That's right, sir.'

'And did he come back later for more drinks?'

'Not to me, sir, but there were three of us serving.'

'Can you describe this gentleman?'

'Mid-forties, dark curly hair, business suit and a rather classy tie.'

Webb let out his breath on a long sigh. 'And the lady?'

'Oh, a bit of all right, sir, if you take my meaning. Blonde hair, green eyes, nice figure. Looked like a model.'

'Have you seen her in here before?'

'Nope.'

'Did you notice who she was with?'

He shook his head. 'Honest, sir, I was run off my feet.'

'But you'd know her again?'

'Not half!' the barman confirmed with a grin. Then suddenly, realizing the direction of the questioning, he sobered. 'You're never saying that's the bloke that died?'

'It seems very likely. What time did all this take place?'

'Sorry, sir, all I can tell you is it was in the lunch hour.'

Their food arrived and Webb nodded to Jackson to take it to an alcove.

'When we've eaten I'd like a word with your two colleagues,' he told the barman.

When Webb reached the table, Jackson was already

tucking into his meal and they ate in companionable silence. Only when they'd finished did Jackson take time to look about him, stroking the rich upholstery on which they sat and gazing admiringly at the bronze horse.

'Lovely statue, that,' he remarked. 'Copper Coin, for a pound.'

'Tut, tut, Ken, I didn't know you were a gambling man.'

'Oh, I'm not, Guv. With a wife and four kids I don't need any help in throwing money away. But there are three races I put a bit on each year—the National, the Derby and the Cup. And that little beauty's won me a bob or two over the years.'

'Excuse me, sir.'

Webb looked up. A man was standing at the table, his bottle-green jacket and bow-tie identifying him as one of the barmen.

'You was asking about a lady in here yesterday? Blonde lady?'

Webb's interest quickened. 'Yes, indeed.'

'Well, sir, she was meeting Mr Derringer, one of our guests. I took their drinks across myself.'

'This Mr Derringer—he isn't a man in his forties, with dark curly hair?' (Could Samantha have misheard 'Kerringer'?)

'Oh no, sir. Fifties at least, and balding.'

Too bad. 'Is he staying here?'

'That's right, sir.'

'And the lady?'

'I've not seen her before.'

'Did you see the other gentleman, with curly hair?'

'Afraid not, sir. We were very busy.'

'Any idea of the approximate time?'

'Oh, I couldn't say. Like Bedlam it was, in here.'

'Well, thanks very much, Mr—?'

'Barker, Sid Barker. Me other mate didn't see neither of them—me and Ted just asked him.'

'I'm grateful for your help, Mr Barker. Thank you.'

As the man moved away, Webb's bleeper sounded, loud in the almost empty bar.

'Good timing,' he continued. 'Sounds as though Stapleton's arrived. I'll go and have a quick word, then we'll track down Mr Derringer.'

The pathologist, who was bending over the figure in the chair, glanced over his shoulder with a grunt as Webb approached, then resumed his examination. He would comment when he was ready, and Webb waited patiently.

Several minutes later, Stapleton straightened. 'Before you ask, Chief Inspector,' he said in his clipped voice, 'time of death could be anything up to twenty-four hours. Rigor mortis is wearing off, as you see, but it would have been accelerated in this heat—the radiator's immediately behind him. No outward marks, at least on preliminary examination. Should be able to tell more when we get him on the slab.'

'And no ID, as you'll have heard.'

'Unusual, I grant you, in these days when we're all tagged and labelled, though personally I see nothing sinister in it. If he hadn't come by car he would not have his driving licence, and as for the ubiquitous credit cards, he might simply not have held with them. I don't myself.'

'You presumably have a cheque-book, though?'

The pathologist took refuge in his habitual grunt. 'There's nothing more I can do here. I'll see you, no doubt, at the mortuary.'

As Webb followed him out of the room the Scenes of Crime officers were arriving. Webb stopped to tell them about the straightened bedspread.

'Otherwise, nothing has been touched as far as I know. The chambermaid said the chair isn't usually turned in to face the table, so if you're lucky you might get some prints off it. Let's hope so, anyway. We could do with a break on this one.'

CHAPTER 5

News of their detention had obviously sifted through to the guests. Little groups were conferring in hallways, some apprehensive, some indignantly looking at their watches, and as Webb and Jackson turned into the lounge they could see a uniformed figure stationed implacably at the front entrance. The net had closed, but was the fish still in it?

Ignoring the agitation around him, Mr Derringer was holding a meeting in one corner of the lounge, and was not pleased at being interrupted. However, the manager's wheedling finally extracted him, and he bustled over to where Webb and Jackson stood waiting.

'I can't imagine what you want with me,' he said crossly. 'I gather one of the guests has died, but why that should necessitate not only my being confined to the building but my clients as well, I simply do not understand. It hardly makes for good business relations.'

The two men with whom Derringer had been talking were staring curiously in their direction. Webb said imperturbably, 'I believe you met a lady in the bar yesterday.'

Derringer reddened, the flush spreading over the polished dome of his head. 'I hope, Chief Inspector, that you're not suggesting anything improper.'

'I'm suggesting nothing at all, sir, merely asking a question.'

'Then yes, I did. That also was a business appointment, but because of the limited time factor it seemed sensible to incorporate lunch. I'm on a tight schedule, as I've already told one of your men.'

'The lady's name, sir?'

'Mrs French, of French Furnishings.'

'*French* Furnishings?'

Derringer said impatiently, 'Merely a play on her name. She's as English as I am.'

'Have you the lady's address, sir?'

'Somewhere, I suppose.' He looked up sharply. 'Why, what has she done? I can't afford to be tied up with anything shady.'

'As far as I know she's done nothing. In fact, it's not the lady herself we're interested in but the gentleman she was speaking to before you arrived.'

'And what do you want *him* for?'

Webb said smoothly, 'We don't want him, sir. In a manner of speaking, we've already got him. It was he who was found dead this morning.'

'Good God. I hadn't realized.'

'You saw him, then?'

'Of course I saw him. He was in one alcove, obviously waiting for someone, and I in another—Mrs French had been delayed. When she came in, she saw him first and approached him by mistake. I overheard her say, "Mr Derringer?" so I made myself known.'

'Did anything strike you about him, sir? His manner or apparent state of mind?'

'I saw that he was getting agitated, presumably because his appointment was overdue. I remember thinking, "You'd better calm down, my boy; if they see you in that state they won't trust your business judgement."'

'In what way did he seem agitated?'

'Oh, constantly looking at his watch and then at the door. And he'd no sooner finished one cigarette than he lit up another.'

Webb nodded. 'And afterwards, when you'd sorted yourselves out, did Mrs French make any comment about him?'

'Only in apologizing for her mistake.'

'Did you notice if this gentleman's friends arrived later?'

'I can't say I did. As soon as we embarked on our business discussion, I forgot about him.'

'What time was your appointment with Mrs French, sir?'

'Twelve-thirty,' Derringer replied promptly, 'but she was at least fifteen minutes late.'

At last they had that tied down.

'Was the other gentleman here when you arrived?'

'No. I can be sure of that because I was keeping an eye open for Mrs French and saw him arrive.'

'What time would that have been?'

'About twelve-forty, I'd say.'

Mention of time had reminded Derringer of its passing and he glanced at his watch. 'Look, there really is nothing else I can tell you, Chief Inspector. Naturally I'm sorry about the death, but there it is. If you want to see Mrs French, the premises are in East Parade, though I doubt if she can help you. Now you really must excuse me.'

Webb let him go; his home address and further details would be noted during a routine interview later.

'East Parade,' Jackson commented. 'Very up-market.'

'And just across the road. Things are under way here so we might as well call on the lady and see what she can tell us about the elusive Mr K.'

French Furnishings was three doors down from Randall Tovey's, the exclusive store which itself had been caught up in violent death a few months previously. The window display was arresting—delicate chairs, an antique chest spilling out brilliantly coloured fabrics, and interestingly shaped vases grouped on an oriental rug. An indication, no doubt, of the comprehensiveness of the service offered.

Webb pushed open the door, and when a girl approached them, asked for the proprietor.

'Have you an appointment, sir?'

'No.' He held up his warrant card. 'DCI Webb and Sergeant Jackson, Shillingham CID.'

She looked startled. 'Mrs French is on the phone, sir. Would you mind waiting a moment?'

'Of course not.'

Webb stood happily enough, looking about him and soaking up atmosphere. The barman had described a glamour-girl, but it seemed she was an astute business-woman. There was constant activity around him as customers compared curtain fabrics, examined delicate lamps, or moved about with cumbersome books of wallpaper, and the assistants were bustling in and out with swatches of material and order books.

Alcoves around the perimeter had been decorated as sections of, respectively, a bedroom, a sitting-room and a dining area, each displaying a flair which appealed to Webb's artistic sensibilities. It certainly seemed a flourishing business, and he was looking forward to meeting its owner.

The phone behind the till rang and the girl beckoned them, leading them to a panelled door at one side of the display area. She tapped on it and stepped aside for them to enter.

Christina came round the side of the desk to greet them, and it was obvious the barman had not exaggerated her attractions. She was not, however, the girl Webb had half-expected, but a woman in her forties, mature and self-confident. Ash-blonde hair hung in a straight silken curtain to the level of her chin and her long, almond-shaped eyes were sea-green. She wore her designer clothes with the careless grace of a model, the knee-length skirt revealing a pair of long, slender legs. Jackson reminded himself that he was a married man and averted his eyes.

'This is most intriguing, Chief Inspector. How can I help you?'

'I believe, Mrs French, that you had a lunch appointment at the King's Head yesterday?'

'Dear me!' she said mockingly. 'Is Big Brother watching me?'

'And,' Webb continued, 'that in the first instance you mistakenly approached the wrong gentleman?'

She waved them to a seat and returned to her own. 'Yes, what of it?'

'Can you give us any information about that gentleman?'

She stared at him for a moment, then said, 'None whatever.'

'He didn't introduce himself?'

'He didn't have the chance. He offered me a drink but

I was still looking round for Mr Derringer. Then almost at once, he came over, and that was that.'

The feeling of let-down told Webb that he'd hoped for more from this meeting.

'You exchanged no personal details whatsoever?'

She frowned at his persistence. 'None. Am I to be told the point of these questions?'

'Did you see him again, after you joined Mr Derringer?'

'Only as he left the bar.'

'Alone?' Webb asked quickly.

'No, with a couple—a man and woman. Look, what is all this?'

'Mrs French, I'm sorry to tell you that the gentleman in question was found dead in his room this morning.'

Watching her, Webb saw her eyes go blank with shock. 'Oh,' she said after a moment. Then, 'I *am* sorry. And you don't know who he is? But surely—'

'Could you describe this couple for me?'

It took her a moment to drag her thoughts from the dead man. 'I caught only a glimpse of them—they were nothing out of the ordinary.'

'Old? Young?'

'About his age. Look, if he was staying at the hotel, they must know who he was.'

'Unfortunately not. The desk was very busy, so he simply took his key and the receptionist can't remember the name he gave.'

'So there's no way of letting his family know? How absolutely terrible. But surely he had papers on him—chequebook—?' Her voice trailed off as Webb shook his head.

She said slowly, 'Isn't that rather strange?'

'Yes, Mrs French, very strange.' Whatever Stapleton might think.

She moistened her lips. 'Chief Inspector, are you saying what I think you're saying?'

'That we suspect foul play? It's on the cards, I'm afraid.'

'My God!' she said softly.

'In which case we might need to call on you again. Could

you give the Sergeant here your full name and address, please?'

She did so.

'What time did you actually arrive at the hotel, Mrs French?'

'Quarter to one. I'd just flown back from Scotland and the shuttle was late.' She paused. 'How did he die?'

'It hasn't been established yet. I'm sorry to press the point, but he didn't say where he'd come from, who he was meeting—? A pity Mr Derringer claimed you so quickly.'

She'd thought the same herself, Christina remembered. And now the man was dead.

Webb rose, signalling to Jackson. 'Well, thank you for your help. Oh—one further point. He didn't happen to have a briefcase with him, did he?'

'Yes, he had. It was propped against his seat. Surely there'll be something in that to identify him?'

'Except,' Webb said deliberately, 'that there was no brief-case in his room.' And leaving her staring after them, he and Jackson took their leave.

When they arrived back at Carrington Street, it was to find a commotion going on in the foyer. The desk sergeant and two other officers were attempting to deal with a couple who appeared on the verge of hysteria.

Webb hesitated, then, catching Andy Fenton's eye, went over to the desk. 'Is there a problem?' he asked.

The woman spun to face him. 'They've stolen my baby, if you call that a problem!' she cried. 'And what's more, you won't do anything to stop them!'

Visions of kidnapping flashed through Webb's mind but Fenton interposed quickly, 'It's not quite what it seems, sir. This lady says a religious sect has alienated her son. I've tried to explain it's a matter for the Special Branch—'

'Which sect would that be?' As if he didn't know, Webb thought resignedly. He'd been waiting for something like this.

'The Final Revelationists or something. They ought to be locked up, poisoning a child's mind against his parents.'

'How old is your son, ma'am?'

'Just had his sixteenth birthday.' It was her husband who replied.

'And they've abducted him?'

'Oh, not *physically*,' the man said with bitterness. 'He's still living at home, going to school and so on. It's his *mind* they've got at. Turned him into a zombie.'

'He was such a bright boy!' the woman sobbed. 'Good at games, played the drums in the school band, lots of friends. Now he just shuts himself away in his room reading their pamphlets and listening to their cassettes, and as fast as I take them away, he gets more. And he tells us the food we eat is "unclean"!' she added, indignation creeping into her voice. 'He won't touch meat or fish any more. I'm at my wits' end, wondering what to get him.'

Webb said gently, 'It's really not a matter for the police, ma'am, not if they haven't physically abducted him. But there are organizations who deal with this. Ask the Citizen's Advice Bureau, they'll tell you about them.'

She was about to argue further, but Webb nodded and walked firmly to the security door, leaving Fenton and the others to get rid of the couple.

'There was something on the Intelligence Bulletin about that lot,' Jackson remarked as they started up the stairs.

'Yep. WDI Petrie went to suss them out last week and didn't like what she saw. It mightn't be a bad idea to have another word with her. Ask her to come to my room when she has a minute, would you, Ken? And get young Marshbanks to go through the telephone directory and list all two-syllable names beginning with K that have an upper-looped letter in the middle.'

'He'll love that,' Jackson said with a grin.

'Then he can take it round to Samantha at the King's Head and see if any of them rings a bell. And I want the hotel guests and staff to identify their cars, so we know if any are unclaimed. Organize it, will you?' And Webb turned into his office and shut the door.

*

Nina received Webb's message with mixed feelings. She'd heard about the scene in the front office and was in no doubt what he wished to speak to her about. The trouble was that she didn't know whether or not she wanted to continue investigating the Revvies. Ever since her visit to Victoria Drive she'd been aware of a niggling wish to return, and the words *love, trust, salvation* still drifted disconcertingly in and out of her mind.

The leaflet she'd been handed on leaving had posed more questions than it answered, but it had sounded the usual dire warnings about the end of the world. Only the Revelationists, it seemed, had any chance of survival. Which, Nina thought with a shrug, was what they all said.

All the same, she'd underestimated the Reverend Noah Bellringer. Whether or not he'd used subliminal means, his message had lodged in the consciousness of a hard-bitten policewoman and, priding herself on her strength of will, the fact both annoyed and intrigued her.

But Webb did not resolve her choice for her. He motioned to her to sit down and said abruptly, 'Nina, I've a lot on, and strictly speaking this Revvie lot is not our concern. But they're on my patch and I imagine we're going to get an increasing number of people coming to complain about them. Can I hand them over to you—unofficially, of course? I want to know what makes them tick, and if we've any excuse for moving them on.'

He looked at her through narrowed eyes. 'Or would you rather not?'

'Quite frankly, sir, I'm not sure. To be honest, I'm a bit apprehensive; they're a persuasive lot, and the last thing you want is a WDI ranting and raving about the end of the world.'

'You think you might be susceptible?'

'Not in the normal way, but if they're using subliminal means, they could convince anyone.' She met his eyes. 'Yes, you're right. Put like that, the threat's obvious. I'll go back.'

'When's the next meeting?'

'Tomorrow evening.'

'You are sure? I don't want to push you into anything you might regret.'

'I'm sure. They need sorting, and I'm in as a good position as any to do it.'

'Well, watch yourself, and if you feel you're getting in over your head, cut and run. Understood?'

'Yes, Guv.'

'Keep me briefed as to how you get on.'

She nodded, and as he gestured in dismissal, left the room. So, one way or another, the die had been cast. She would attend an instruction session and see what that led to. And, she thought before she could stop herself, she would see Daniel again.

Webb's phone rang and he reached for it absent-mindedly. It was the editor of the *Broadshire Evening News*.

'Yes, Mike, what can I do for you?'

'Just wondering if you've any titbits about the stiff at the King's Head?'

'There's a press conference at five.'

'Oh, come on, Dave! I've got an evening paper to get out!'

'Actually we know very little—not even who he is. No papers on him, and all we've got is that although he himself was English, his clothes were made in France. Appeared at the King's Head out of the blue, didn't check in because of the crush at the desk, and popped his clogs before he'd a chance to remedy it. Oh, and he went to the bar, and was seen leaving with a man and a woman.'

'Who you're hoping will come forward?'

'We should be so lucky.'

'It wasn't a natural death, then?'

'I'm off to the PM now, after which I hope to know more.'

'Well, thanks. Oh, and while you're on, any cartoons for me?'

Webb grimaced. 'If you're going to start nagging, I'll hang up.'

'Come on, it's months since we had any. Someone even wrote in asking what had happened to them.'

Webb's gift for drawing pungent cartoons was a well-kept secret, since he signed them merely with an S in a circle—symbolizing a spider in a web. More importantly, he used his knack of caricature to depict suspects in his inquiries. By setting out his players on the stage of his canvas, he could place them where they stated they'd been at a crucial time, and seeing the overall picture in black and white showed up inconsistencies which sometimes proved vital. On other occasions, the amazingly life-like figures alerted him to some trait of character which he'd initially registered only subconsciously.

'There are probably some in my drawer,' he said resignedly.

'Good lad. Let me have them, then. And we must have a drink sometime.'

Webb grunted noncommittally, put down the phone and, with the familiar sinking feeling in his stomach, set off to attend the post-mortem.

Hannah sat at her desk at Ashbourne School, gazing meditatively into space. She really couldn't delay speaking to Miss Hendrix any longer; she was looking more and more threadbare, and at lunch-time Hannah had overheard two of the girls giggling about her in the corridor.

The worry was how to broach the subject without hurting her feelings. Still, things wouldn't improve by any further delay—she'd procrastinated long enough. Sighing, she reached for the telephone, and as she did so it started to ring.

'Hello?'

'Mr Frobisher is here, Miss James. Could you spare him a moment?'

Relief flooded over her. Charles Frobisher, Chairman of the Board of Governors, was an old friend. He'd a sensible head on his shoulders—she could discuss the problem with him.

'Of course, Amanda. Show him in—and would you bring us some tea?'

When the secretary had closed the door, Charles came over and kissed Hannah's cheek. 'How are you, my dear? The trappings of power going to your head?'

'Far from it. It's good to see you, particularly as I could do with some advice.'

'Always glad to help, you know that.'

Hannah, feeling better already, regarded him with affection. Twelve years a widower, he was, she knew, fond of her. There had been a time when she'd contemplated marrying him—and she could have done a lot worse. But when it came to the point she'd been unable to dismiss David Webb from her life, flexible though their relationship was.

Charles was watching her, his lean, clever face speculative, and she felt herself flush, wondering how many of her thoughts he'd been able to read. Fortunately, Amanda Grant came to her rescue with the tea, and in the business of pouring it, any remaining tension was dissolved.

'First though, tell me to what I owe this honour,' she prompted, handing him a cup and saucer.

'When we last met, if you remember, I invited you to the Golf Club Dinner. You were going to let me know if you could make it.'

Hannah was overcome with guilt. He had indeed mentioned the dinner, several weeks ago, and she'd delayed giving him an answer partly because she was unsure what lay behind the invitation. Was it, as it seemed on the surface, quite straightforward with no strings attached? Or had Charles decided it was time to renew his attentions, as he'd warned her he would?

She looked up, catching his eye, and again had the impression he knew what she was thinking. 'I'm so sorry, Charles. I have to confess it went straight out of my head.'

Which was hardly tactful, as she immediately realized. However, he merely smiled and said, 'Well, time's moving

on; it's a week on Friday, the 22nd. I think you'd enjoy it;
John and Beatrice will be at our table—and it would do
you good to be seen about more socially.'

'You make it sound as though I'm in purdah,' she protested, but she knew what he meant. During their time
together, she had enjoyed the dinners, concerts and theatres
to which he had escorted her. It was a style of life to which
David, with his erratic work schedule, seldom managed to
conform, and with Gwen now abroad and Monica married,
most of her social activities consisted of dinner or the
theatre with Dilys which, much as she enjoyed them, had
their limitations. If Charles would only accept a platonic
basis, she'd be delighted to accompany him more often.

In this instance, though, she now had no choice. 'I'm so
sorry not to have come back to you, but I am free that
evening and I'd be delighted to go.'

'Good. That's settled, then. Now, what was this advice
you were after?'

Hannah switched her mind from personal to professional
problems. 'It's about a member of staff.' And she explained
about Mattie Hendrix.

'She goes round looking like a tramp,' she ended, 'and I
can see no possible reason for it. She's on a good salary
and has no dependants.'

Charles thought for a moment. 'How long has she been
here?'

'Since September last year.'

'And before that?'

'St Anne's, Erlesborough.'

'You know their headmistress, don't you?'

'Marion Bowles? Yes, of course.'

'Why not give her a ring and ask in confidence if she
noticed anything odd about her?'

'That might be an idea.'

'If she didn't, you'd have to look for a more recent cause.
You say this woman has no dependants—where does she
live?'

'I think she has a bedsit somewhere.'

'Does she share it with anyone?'

'Not that I know of, though it's possible—I did see her with a woman in town the other day. I'm ashamed to say, Charles, I know very little about her. She's not forthcoming, and there's a limit to the casual questions you can ask.'

'Any complaints about her work?'

'Positively not. She's an excellent teacher.'

'Does she drink?'

Hannah looked startled. 'I don't think so.'

'It would account for shortage of money, that's all. Booze or drugs.'

'Oh, I don't—' Hannah began, then broke off. Now that she thought about it, there *was* sometimes an unfocused look about Miss Hendrix, and as she'd remarked to Dilys, she was a bundle of nerves. 'Oh Lord, I do hope not. That I could do without.'

'What age is she?'

'Late thirties. It was Gwen who engaged her, of course, which is why I don't want her taking offence and waltzing off while I'm holding the fort.'

'If you think she's bringing the school into disrepute, you've no option but to say something.'

'Oh, that's a bit strong,' Hannah demurred. 'No one seeing her round town would know she teaches at Ashbourne.'

'But there are Parents' Evenings, concerts and so on. And what impression would she make on prospective parents being shown round the school?'

Hannah sighed. 'You're right, of course. She's becoming an embarrassment, and the girls are starting to make fun of her.'

'Which last, I imagine, is an occupational hazard,' Charles commented drily.

There was a scratching at the window, and Hannah went to let her cat in. Purring loudly, he proceeded to wind himself round her legs, impeding her return to the desk.

'He knows when it's tea-time,' she said, taking a dish from a drawer and pouring milk into it. She set it on the carpet and the cat walked casually over, then settled on its hunkers and began to lap delicately.

Charles watched it for a moment. 'Well, I must be on my way and let you get on with your work. I'll phone nearer the time about arrangements for the 22nd.'

'Right.' She walked with him to the door. 'Thanks for your advice, I'll let you know how I get on.'

All the same, she wished Gwen were here. Dear Gwen: Hannah conjured her up in her mind, the earnest brown eyes, the tall, gauche frame and untidy hair. Only those who knew her were aware that the diffident exterior concealed a brilliant academic brain.

Hannah stood for a moment watching the cat who, having finished the milk, was engaged in a full-scale washing operation. She'd have a word with Miss Hendrix first, she decided. Then, if things didn't improve, she'd phone Marion Bowles. But Charles's visit had delayed her; it was now after four, school was over for the day and everyone would be going their separate ways. It would after all be necessary to hold it over for another day.

Across the town, Webb pushed his way into his office and flopped into his chair. DI Crombie surveyed him over the top of his spectacles.

'Fresh from the abattoir?'

'Too right. I'll never get used to it—the smell of that disinfectant gets right up my nose.'

'Better than other smells,' said Crombie judiciously. 'And what did old Stapleton come up with?'

'I knew this was going to be stinker, Alan, right from the start. It has to be a fatal injection, but there are no traces of poison in the body.'

Crombie raised an eyebrow. 'You found the puncture mark?'

'Only by the grace of God, because the bloke bruised easily. There was a tiny purple mark on his upper arm. Since he would hardly have let them undress him, it must have gone through his clothes.

'Stapleton's reluctant to commit himself, as always, but he's leaning towards curare, which is quickly broken down and leaves little or no evidence. There was petechial hæmorrhaging, which seems to support it. Anyway, tests are continuing.'

'Well, it makes a change from the old blunt instrument,' Crombie commented.

'True; we have all the signs of premeditation and not a suspect in sight. What's more, we're still no nearer finding out who he is. Let's hope the telexes produce some result.'

CHAPTER 6

'Chief Inspector Webb?'

'Speaking.' Webb recognized the voice of the hotel manager.

'Jeffrey Diccon here. Something has come up which might interest you. Now that we can get into 251 again, the chambermaid has checked the mini-bar and some bottles are missing.'

Webb frowned. 'What exactly are you saying, Mr Diccon?'

'Well, Maggie—the chambermaid—said you asked if there were glasses on the table and she said no. But they must have had drinks after all, and—and someone washed the glasses and put them back in the bar.'

Webb pursed his lips. A cool customer indeed. 'There's no possibility of a mistake?'

'No, sir. The bar is checked each morning, and any used items are entered on the guest's bill and replaced.'

'What bottles are missing?'

'A whisky, a white wine and a beer.'

'But there were no empties in the bin?'

'It seems not. Maggie certainly didn't remove any.' He hesitated. 'I thought maybe if—if he was poisoned—'

'Yes, indeed. Good of you to let me know. The maid didn't touch any of the glasses?'

'No, but they were all there.'

With no glasses out, the SOCOs wouldn't have bothered with the mini-bar. A return visit was called for, though if the murderers were that careful, they were unlikely to have left fingerprints.

'Excellent. Then would you lock the room again till some-one can take another look? And many thanks for your help.'

He was about to replace the phone, but the man was still speaking. 'I saw the item in last night's *News*. Has anyone rung in to identify him?'

'There've been several suggestions, we're still sorting through them. Thanks for calling, Mr Diccon.'

If the poison had been ingested, Webb reflected, the information could have been crucial. At least it explained the lack of glasses, which had puzzled him at the time; if K and the others left the bar to go to his room, the natural thing would have been to have drinks there. But *why* had they gone upstairs? At that time of day the restaurant would have been a more natural venue. Had K something to show them? If so, it wasn't in the missing briefcase—he'd had that with him in the bar.

There was a knock on the door and DC Marshbanks put his head round it.

'Have you got a minute, Guv?'

'Of course, Simon. What is it?'

'I went through the Ks yesterday, like you said, but when I got to the King's Head Samantha wasn't on duty. So I've just been back now.'

'And?'

'Well, she hesitated for a while over Kirby and Kerley but now she thinks it might have been Kershaw.'

'Hardly a positive ID.'

'Sorry, sir. The best she could come up with.'

'All right, Simon, thanks.'

Webb stared down at the papers in front of him, mentally ticking off each action taken. A dental chart of the deceased

had been telexed to all UK dentists and a copy sent to
Interpol for circulation in France. His full description had
gone to all police stations in the UK and also to Interpol,
and a mug shot was already up in the foyer downstairs,
below the caption DO YOU KNOW THIS MAN? Mean-
while the support group were still working their way
through the hotel guests.

They were due for a break, he thought, and as if in answer
the phone rang again. It was the Met.

'Regarding your telex, sir, we've had a call from a local
wine company reporting a missing employee, and the
description seems to fit. They held a conference during the
weekend which this man attended, but he's based in France
and their French office has been on to them to say he's not
returned home.'

'Have you a name for him, Inspector?'

'Philip Kershaw.'

'Bingo! That was one of the options we came up with.
Right, now, if you can give me the name and address of
the wine company, I'll send someone along.'

He wrote it down, the phone cradled under his chin.
'That's our first break, Inspector. I'm much obliged.'

Dropping the phone back on its hook, he strode to the
door and yelled 'Don! In here at the double!'

Sergeant Partridge was in the room before Webb
regained his desk. 'Yes, Guv?'

'We've had a break from the Met. One Philip Kershaw,
working for a wine company and based in France, gone
AWOL. He attended a conference in London over the
weekend, and I want you to get up there and interview as
many of his colleagues as you can trace. Take John Manning with you. We want anything you can get—contacts,
habits, hobbies, state of his marriage, the lot.'

He tore the top sheet off his pad and handed it over.
'Here's the address. Report back as soon as you have
anything.'

Partridge nodded and hurried out of the office. Webb
glanced at his watch. Getting on for midday. He'd collect

Ken and go along to the hotel. With luck the interviews might have turned up something interesting.

Hannah sat at her desk gazing helplessly at Miss Hendrix's bent head. The woman seemed positively cowed, she thought. On this bright autumn day she was dressed in a dusty-looking black skirt with an uneven hemline and a cable-knit maroon sweater of uncertain years. The front of it was matted with too much washing and the sleeves, obviously too long, had been turned back to form unwieldy cuffs.

But quite apart from her clothes, the woman looked *ill*, Hannah thought with consternation. Had she always been so pale, with such dark shadows under her eyes, her cheeks so hollow and her chin so pointed?

'Miss Hendrix,' she said gently, 'is anything troubling you?'

Mattie looked up, startled. When summoned to Miss James's study she had anticipated a discussion on the progress of her pupils, or some news about the proposed end of term readings. She was not prepared for a personal interrogation.

'How do you mean, Miss James?' she stammered.

'Well, you seem so—pale, and I noticed in the dining-hall the other day you scarcely ate anything. I know you don't take meat—are you sure you're getting enough protein?'

Mattie Hendrix forced a smile. 'My diet is perfectly adequate, thank you, Miss James, and nothing is troubling me. In fact,' she added for good measure, 'I have never felt happier.'

Hannah was slightly taken aback. 'Well, I'm glad to hear it.' She paused, wondering how to raise the subject which really concerned her. 'Forgive me, but are you finding it difficult to manage on your salary? Because if so, I'm sure—'

'Why should you think that?'

To her annoyance, Hannah felt herself flush. 'Well, I—'

But her glance had been more eloquent than she realized. Mattie looked down at her skirt as though noticing it for the first time. 'I see,' she said, under her breath. 'I'm sorry, Miss James, I hadn't realized. I'm not interested in clothes, but I try to keep neat and tidy. Obviously I haven't succeeded.'

'It's just that when parents come—'

'Of course. My appearance reflects badly on the school. It was thoughtless of me and I apologize.'

'But if money's a problem,' Hannah began, while wondering how it could possibly be, 'we could discuss—'

'I have enough for my needs, thank you. You won't have any further cause for complaint.'

'Thank you,' Hannah said weakly, balked in her attempts to find the cause of such apparent poverty. Mattie Hendrix rose to go and Hannah said on impulse, 'There is one thing you could help me on, if you would. Two of the girls came back from *exeat* saying they've become vegetarians. Could you perhaps guide them into eating the right things to keep up their strength? I'd be so grateful. They're—'

'Stephanie French and Marina Chase.'

Hannah looked up in surprise. 'You've noticed already?'

'No, but I guessed,' Mattie replied inscrutably, and left the room leaving Hannah frowning after her. What did she mean, she'd guessed? How could you *guess* a particular girl had turned vegetarian?

Hannah sighed. Well, at least she'd broached the subject of Miss Hendrix's clothes, apparently without giving offence. She hoped fervently that that would be the end of the matter.

The headquarters of the wine company was in south-west London, off the Old Brompton Road. DC Manning parked directly outside on the yellow line, propping his log book on the dashboard for any marauding traffic warden.

They got out of the car and stood looking up at the imposing building. 'Reckon we might get a free sample to take home, Skip?' Manning asked with a grin.

'Doubtful in the extreme,' replied Partridge. 'But at the moment I'd settle for a cuppa.'

They went up the broad steps into the foyer of the building, and minutes later were shown into the office of Mr Ray, the managing director. He was a small, round man with an entirely bald head which distractingly mirrored the overhead light.

'This is a great shock, gentlemen,' he greeted them, shaking them gravely by the hand. 'A great shock. Please take a seat and tell me how I may help you.'

'Well, sir, since we've only just been able to identify Mr Kershaw, we know nothing whatever about him and would be grateful for anything you can tell us.'

'Let me see, then. He's worked for us for about fifteen years now, a very able, conscientious man and a leading authority on Loire wines. He married a French girl—in fact, the daughter of one of our suppliers—and lives—lived in the Loire valley. He comes to London every three months or so.'

'When did he arrive on this latest visit?'

'Friday evening. The usual reservations had been made for him and several other overseas staff who were attending the conference.'

'Have you any idea how he spent the evening?'

'I'm afraid not. My staff might know.'

'Were you aware of any family problems—marital difficulties, things of that kind?'

Mr Ray shook his head. 'To the best of my knowledge he was happily married, with a young daughter.'

'When did the conference end?'

'At lunch-time on Sunday.'

'So when would you have expected him to return to France?'

'I should have thought that evening, but I was speaking to one of my managers, who said Kershaw told him he was staying on a couple of days to attend to some family business.'

'Did he say where that was?'

'In your neck of the woods, I believe.'

Partridge said diffidently, 'Someone will have to identify him, and it seems hard to bring his wife over from France. Do you think—?'

The man's ruddy cheeks paled slightly, but after a pause he nodded. 'Yes, of course; it's the least I can do.'

'Thank you, sir. We'll be in touch to arrange a convenient time.'

There was little more he could tell them, and his secretary escorted the detectives down the corridor to another office where two men awaited them with obvious apprehension. Jack Spedding and Rick Burgess had spent some time with Kershaw during the conference and were clearly shaken by his death.

'How did he seem?' Partridge asked them when they had seated themselves and Manning had fished out his notebook again.

'Fairly cheerful,' Spedding replied. 'He was an affable chap, though unforthcoming on personal matters. Would tell a story with the best of them, but never exchanged confidences, the way a lot of the lads do after the odd bottle of wine.'

'Was he happily married, would you say?'

'Oh, no doubt of that. You could tell by the way he spoke of her. Cracker of a girl she is, too. And he thought the world of his daughter.'

Not much to go on there. 'What about his interests outside work—hobbies and so on?'

The two men looked at each other and shrugged. 'Played a bit of golf, I think,' Spedding said.

'And a mean hand of poker!' Burgess added with a grin. 'Many a night I've sat up with him after a dinner, and it never did me any good.'

'Did you on Saturday?'

'Yes, I did, as a matter of fact, with some of the other lads.'

'Did he win?'

'I'll say. Hands down.'

'Anyone lose heavily to him?'

Burgess met his eyes. 'Not heavily enough to kill for.'

'Was he a serious gambler, would you say?' Partridge's mind was on moneylenders.

'I couldn't say, with him being over in France, but he certainly liked his game.'

'He told you he was staying on to attend to family business?'

'That's right. His mother died a few weeks ago and there were things to see to at the house.'

'Which was where, Mr Spedding?'

'In Shillingham, I think. He wasn't looking forward to going through her things, and said that rather than spend the night in the cold house he'd book into an hotel.' He made a grimace. 'Seems he chose the wrong one.'

'Can you think why anyone should have wanted to kill him?'

'Lord, no! I mean, he wasn't likely to have been messing round with anyone's wife, or anything like that. And our line of business doesn't usually bring out the long knives.'

'Do you know how he spent Friday evening?'

'With the other overseas chaps, at the hotel. They all had dinner together.'

'Which hotel was that?'

'The Commodore, in Cresswell Gardens—just round the corner.'

Which was their next port of call. In response to their inquiries, they learned not only that Kershaw had made a phone-call from his room, but also, thanks to the hotel's call-logging equipment, the number dialled, which was a Shillingham one. For the rest, he had left the hotel soon after breakfast on Monday morning and the hall porter, who had seen him into a taxi, heard him ask for Paddington Station.

'Right, John, let's head for home,' Partridge said. 'With luck we'll just miss the rush-hour.'

*

Nina was unprepared for the warmth of her welcome when she returned to Victoria Drive that evening. Again, it was Sarah who opened the door, and her sombre face lit up.

'Nina—how lovely!' she exclaimed, stepping aside and gesturing her in. Top marks for remembering her name, at any rate. 'We're just having coffee before we start.'

Here we go again, thought Nina as she smiled noncommittally. No pomegranate seeds, that was the rule, though it would be difficult to fend off the repeated offers. A pretended allergy to tea or coffee, perhaps. But then they'd offer soft drinks—even water, probably, if they were determined to entrap her.

'Nina!' Daniel came hurrying along the passage, and thoughts of entrapment seemed all at once far-fetched. 'How are you? I'm so glad you could come.'

Perhaps, Nina thought drily a moment later, their pleasure in seeing her was due to the fact that not many people had turned up. There were only about twenty in the back room, standing in the usual awkward little groups with their polystyrene cups.

'Are you expecting any more?' Nina asked Daniel, shaking her head as he tried to hand her a coffee.

'It depends. There's always a fall-out after the initial meeting, which is as it should be. Some people come simply out of curiosity, others feel unable to make a commitment. That's fine. The ones we want are those who've had time to think things over and decide to come back and learn more. I hoped you'd be one of them.' And he smiled warmly into her eyes.

He reminded her of her ex-husband, Nina realized with a slight sense of shock. Ross, too, possessed that easy charm, that way of looking at you as though you were the only woman in the world. Perhaps that's why Daniel attracted her. It was an uncomfortable thought, and she was pleased when someone called her name and she could turn away. It was Pam, with whom she'd sat before.

'Hello, Nina, I was hoping you'd be here!' And she came over to join her.

'Did you tell your husband you were coming this time?' Nina asked her.

'No fear, I'd never hear the end of it. I waited till he went to the pub, and just slipped out. I'll be back before he is, but even if he finds out, I'll still come. I've been looking forward to this ever since Friday.'

If Pam's welcome had been as warm as her own—and she didn't doubt it—it was no wonder she felt at home. Probably more notice had been taken of her by these relative strangers than her family had shown in years. Which, Nina thought, looking round the room, was probably true of most of them. She'd read of this technique the cults adopted—love-bombing, wasn't it?—whereby everyone was made to feel wanted. Well, it seemed to work. She'd even proved susceptible herself.

Although there were several faces she knew from Friday, Nina was relieved that the schoolgirls were not among them. Perhaps their interest had been only a flash in the pan. There were also some people she'd not seen before, among them a tall, broad-shouldered man with an attractive craggy face and an air of authority that aroused her interest.

'Who's that, do you know?' she asked Pam, unconsciously interrupting her flow of chat.

'Brad Lübekker—I was introduced to him a few minutes ago. He's an American, from London. One of the group, and quite high up, I think. No doubt come to give us the once-over!'

Daniel clapped his hands and the chatter died away as they turned expectantly towards him. The tall American moved to his side. 'Hello, everyone, it's great to see you again. I'd like to introduce you to Brad Lübekker here. He is an Elder in our Movement, in charge of all the units in the south-west of England. During the evening he hopes to have a word with everybody.'

'What did I tell you?' whispered Pam in Nina's ear.

'In the meantime, we're going through now for another short talk by Captain Bellringer, after which we'll divide into groups and begin to get to know each other. So if you'd like to come along, we can get started.'

Obediently they filed into the corridor and through a door they hadn't used before which led into the platform end of the meeting room, where the screen was set up. This time, however, the divider had been drawn across the large room, making two smaller ones.

As they settled in their seats and the lights went down, Nina tensed. After the disillusionment of listening to Bellringer's speech with her mother, she was determined not to be hoodwinked again. But the minute the kindly face appeared on screen and the slow, soothing voice flowed over her, she relaxed in spite of herself.

'Hi there!' he began, setting the informal tone of the evening. 'Good to see you again. This evening is a momentous landmark in your lives, my friends, for together we are going to take the first, tentative steps towards salvation.'

Nina made a heroic effort to free herself from the soporific effect of his words but her mind was filled with images of deep, crystal-clear pools, of running water, wooded pathways. Relax, a voice said insistently inside her, there's nothing to worry about. Everything is taken care of.

She shook herself and sat up straighter, scrutinizing the screen for the subliminal messages she was sure were bombarding them. But if they existed, they were too swift for her consciousness to register. He was talking of mountains, of a shining new Jerusalem, of their survival when the rest of the earth perished. None of it made sense, yet all of it did. She just wanted him to go on talking, so that she needn't think, or make decisions, or worry about anything at all.

Then it was over, the screen faded and the lights came on again. For a moment or two there was silence. Then Daniel, who this evening had been sitting in the front row with Lübekker and the other three leaders, got to his feet and turned to face them.

'Now, I'd like you to divide yourselves into four groups. Sarah and I will take two into the front room and the other two will stay here with Adam and Mattie. We'll come together later for a general discussion.'

He walked past them to the divider and opened a small door in it. Nina, still bemused, followed him towards the opening. When she stepped through it, she thought confusedly, what other threshold might she be crossing? She was about to find out.

CHAPTER 7

When Partridge made his report the next morning, Webb checked the phone number Kershaw had dialled from his hotel. Learning that it belonged to a firm of solicitors in Franklyn Road, he decided to walk round and inform them of the death of their client. In return, he hoped for some much-needed reciprocal information.

In this he was disappointed. Though the name on the plate read Culpepper, Soames and Soames, it transpired that Mr Culpepper had died ten years previously and the elder Mr Soames, with whom, according to his desk diary, Kershaw had had an appointment on Monday morning, had left the following day for a walking holiday in Scotland. Nor was his secretary available, being confined to bed with 'flu.

Which left Webb little choice but to conduct his interview with Mr Soames junior, a raw young man in his midtwenties, who was clearly shaken to learn that the man whose murder he'd read about was the son of a client and had, moreover, visited his father on the day of his death.

Under Webb's prompting, he confirmed that Mrs Evelyn Kershaw of Calder's Close had died three weeks ago and that they were administering her estate. However, to his embarrassment, he was unable to produce her will. It appeared Mr Soames senior kept his clients' wills in a small safe in his office, to which his son did not have access.

'I'm so sorry, Chief Inspector,' he said, 'but you see, I

deal with a different side of the practice—legal aid and so on. I don't even know where my father keeps the key.'

Yet another stalemate. Webb considered the position. This was the only lead they had locally; Soames had met Kershaw, who had been killed an hour or so later, and then promptly disappeared 'on holiday'. Careful questioning, however, revealed that the break had been planned for some weeks and that Soames's wife had accompanied him.

Could they have been the couple Mrs French saw with Kershaw? It seemed unlikely. Why, after an interview with him that morning, should Kershaw expect Soames at the hotel? Unless he'd invited him and his wife for lunch?

'Did your father have a lunch appointment on Monday?' Webb inquired. The young man didn't know and the diary was no help.

Webb sighed. 'Are there any other members of the Kershaw family?' he asked, with a hint of desperation. 'Brothers or sisters, uncles, aunts, cousins?'

'No, Mrs Kershaw had no one but her son.'

'And he lived in France.' Poor, lonely old woman. 'What's happening to the family home?'

'It's just been put on the market. I believe that was one of the things they discussed.'

'Is it empty at the moment?'

'Yes, the housekeeper-companion moved out last week.'

'Ah!' He should have realized there'd be a housekeeper. 'Do you know where she went?'

'To her sister's, I think Father said. He made a note of the address—it might be in the file.'

It was, affording Webb his only piece of luck so far that morning. He wrote down the name and address, slipped his notebook into his pocket and stood up. 'Thanks for your help, Mr Soames. If you should hear from your father, please ask him to contact me. And I'd be glad to know when his secretary's back at work—she might know where the key to the safe is.'

As Soames showed him to the door, he added as an

afterthought, 'Did your father make any comment after Mr Kershaw had left?'

'Yes, he said, "Thank God I'm going on holiday tomorrow!" I asked what was wrong, but he just shook his head and went back into his office.'

Webb nodded and went thoughtfully down the steps to the street.

Rankin Close, where the housekeeper was staying, was the other side of town, and Webb returned to Carrington Street to collect Jackson and the car before making his way there. During the drive, he filled him in both with Partridge's findings and what he'd learned himself that morning.

'I've sent Trent to the station to check on taxis,' he finished. 'With luck, someone will remember picking Kershaw up and where he was dropped. No doubt it was either at his mother's or the solicitors', but we might as well be sure.'

He stared out of the window. The trees in Central Gardens were resplendent with autumn foliage, their colours ranging from vermilion to palest gold. Normally, the artist in Webb delighted in them; today he barely noticed them.

'What we're faced with, Ken,' he continued, 'is that Kershaw was killed by someone who'd known not only that he was in Shillingham that day, but at which hotel. Since he hadn't booked in advance, that could only be someone he spoke to after he arrived there. We must get on to the King's Head and see if he made any calls from his room.'

'His work-mates knew he was going to a hotel, according to Don.'

'But not which one. They could have made an informed guess, I suppose, or even rung round till they located him— something else to check with the King's Head. Anyway, they'll be investigated as a matter of routine, though Don seems to have written them off.'

Jackson said thoughtfully, 'Even though he hadn't booked, he might have let it drop to the solicitor. Said something like, "If there's anything else I'll be at the King's

Head." He was surprised to find they were busy, remember; it wouldn't have occurred to him that he mightn't get a room.'

'Good point, Ken. Come to that, he could have said the same thing to anyone.'

'On the other hand, someone could have followed him over from France,' Jackson went on. 'Someone he owed money, perhaps.'

'And a gambling debt led to his death? It's possible. Inquiries are under way at clubs both here and in France, so we'll see what we come up with.'

They had turned into Rankin Close. 'By the way, Guv, DI Petrie was looking for you,' Jackson remembered, as they drew up outside the bungalow.

To report on the previous evening's goings-on, no doubt. 'I'll see her when we get back,' Webb said, pushing open the gate.

Their ring at the bell was answered by a small, neat woman in her forties who smiled at them inquiringly.

'Good morning, ma'am. DCI Webb and Sergeant Jackson, Shillingham CID. Could we have a word with Miss Margaret Preston?'

An expression of slight alarm crossed her face. 'I'm Margaret Preston. Is anything wrong?'

He'd have to break the news to her, too. Webb hoped another death wouldn't be too much for her, coming so soon after her employer's.

He made no reply, merely stepping into the hallway with Jackson at his heels. A woman appeared at the kitchen door and Miss Preston said quickly, 'It's all right, Nora, it's for me.'

She led them into the small front room, pleasantly furnished with a flowered three-piece suite, and gestured to them to be seated. Then, seeming to brace herself, asked steadily, 'Now, Chief Inspector, what's happened?'

'I believe you were companion to the late Mrs Kershaw?'

'That's right.'

'Her son, Mr Philip Kershaw, was over earlier this week. Did he contact you?'

'No.' The word was said quietly, without embellishment or any change in tone, but Webb sensed antagonism behind it. Which might possibly make his task easier.

'Had you known he was coming?'

'No,' she said again. Then, the brevity of her response seeming to strike her, she added, 'But there was no reason for him to get in touch.'

'How long were you with Mrs Kershaw, Miss Preston?'

'Almost six years.'

'So you must have met her son frequently?'

This time she flushed. 'Forgive me, Chief Inspector, but what's the purpose of all these questions?'

'You might have read in the paper of the man found dead at the King's Head?'

'Yes?' Her eyes widened. 'You're surely not saying—?'

'I'm afraid it was Mr Kershaw.'

She stared at him, one hand going to her throat. Then she said softly, 'Thank God his mother was spared that.' She moistened her lips. 'But I got the impression from the reports that—that the death wasn't natural?'

'That's right, Miss Preston. Mr Kershaw was poisoned. Which is why we're trying to trace his movements on Monday morning.'

'But that's terrible! Who would want to murder him?'

'That,' Webb said drily, 'is what we're trying to find out.' He paused. 'Were Mrs Kershaw and her son close?'

Miss Preston was silent. Then she said, 'Oh dear.'

'They weren't?'

'No. There was some terrible quarrel years ago—I don't know what it was about. But to the best of my knowledge, during the six years I was with her there was no contact between them at all.'

A right turn-up for the book, Jackson thought, steadily making his notes.

'Did she speak of him?'

'Never. When I first arrived, she informed me that she

had a son who lived in France, but they were estranged and she didn't wish to speak of him. Naturally, I abided by that.'

'So you know nothing about him at all?'

'Not even what he looked like. There were no photographs, at least on display.'

Nowt stranger than folk, Webb reflected, and how many sides there were to one person. According to Partridge, Kershaw's business colleagues had considered him 'affable', and he was apparently devoted to his wife and child. Mrs French had been genuinely shocked by his death—he'd formed the impression that she found him attractive—and even the receptionist, Samantha, thought him pleasant in her brief contact with him. Yet he had not spoken to his mother for at least six years—possibly much longer. Who had been at fault, Kershaw himself or a possibly domineering and stubborn old woman?

Pursuing that line of thought, Webb asked abruptly, 'What was she like, the old lady?'

'Pleasant.' Miss Preston smiled slightly and added, 'As long as she had her own way. But then why shouldn't she? She was comfortably off and had no one else to consider.'

'Did you ever wonder about that quarrel with her son?'

'I wouldn't have been human if I hadn't, Chief Inspector, but there was no one else to ask about it.'

'Might she have been at least partially to blame?'

'Oh, I don't doubt it. And if he was as strong-willed as she was, neither of them would have made the first move.' She paused. 'You know, it always upsets me, hearing those SOS messages on the radio. Would Mr So-and-so, who hasn't seen his father for twelve years, please get in touch because the old man is dangerously ill. I used to wonder how families could split and lose track of each other so completely, but since going to Mrs Kershaw's, I've seen how it can happen. Though it doesn't make it any less sad.'

'He came over for her funeral, though?'

'No. It was really that which I couldn't forgive, whatever had gone before. He sent flowers, that was all. There were only half a dozen of us there, including Mr Soames, her solicitor.'

Webb shifted on his chair. 'Do you know the terms of the will?'

'Only that she left me very well provided for.'

'She was a wealthy woman?'

'Fairly, I should say.'

'But you've no idea where the bulk of her estate went?'

She shook her head.

Interesting. Very interesting.

Webb nodded to Jackson. 'Thank you for your time, Miss Preston. It has been most helpful.'

'What do you make of that, Guv?' Jackson asked, as they drove away.

'For one thing, I intend to make every effort to track down Mr Soames in the Highlands or wherever he is. He'll have been a confidant of the old biddy—that type always like to have their solicitors dancing attendance. He'll be able to shed more light on her affairs, and particularly on her will. The big question is, did she or didn't she leave it to her errant son? And if she did, who would inherit on his death?'

Dilys sat motionless at her desk, staring through the window at the walnut tree. It was forty-eight hours since the baby and his nanny had arrived at the house, and in that time she had written not one word.

Not that it was their fault. At any rate, not directly. As Susie had promised, the nanny kept to herself and Sebastian had cried only once. He was a good little thing, as babies went. Yet ever since their arrival she had felt on edge, distinctly ill at ease, and she couldn't imagine why.

Impatiently, she pushed her chair back and walked to the French doors from where, at the bottom of the garden, she could see the pram rocking gently under the apple tree. Yet not a sound reached her. Almost she wished it would, to give her a concrete cause for her distraction.

Where was Miss Baines, she wondered. (She still could

not think of her as Sarah.) She'd gone out last night—to
her cousin's, according to Peggy, who had volunteered to
listen for the baby.

And that, thought Dilys irritably, was another thing.
Peggy had defected. One glance at the smoothly rounded
cheeks and guileless blue eyes had been enough to set her
cooing, touching the little fists and trying to coax a smile.
But Sebastian, like his nanny, Dilys suspected, smiled only
when it suited him.

She sighed heavily and turned from the window, trying
to draw comfort and inspiration from this room tailored so
specifically to her needs. An entire wall was given over to
bookshelves, of which her own offerings, in varying editions
and a dozen different languages, accounted for several.
Below them her carefully acquired reference books sat
smugly, confident of their omniscience, while less worthy
but no less loved editions of detective stories, travel books,
French poetry and childhood favourites jostled together in
happy equanimity. Today they failed to soothe her. Dilys
eyed them sourly and turned away.

Aimlessly, she walked through the sitting-room into the
hall and stood listening. She could hear Peggy, who was
cleaning the silver, singing softly to herself in the kitchen.
Obviously she was alone. Impelled by something stronger
than curiosity, Dilys started softly up the stairs, and, half-
ashamed of herself, came to a halt outside the guest-room
door. Holding her breath she stood for a moment listening,
but all she could hear was the occasional rustle of paper.

Making up her mind, and after only the briefest of
knocks, she opened the door. Sarah Baines turned sharply
towards her. She was seated at the dressing-table, which
had been cleared of its usual trinkets and was covered with
orderly piles of paper and open text books. There was a
pen in her hand.

'Oh, there you are,' Dilys said pleasantly. 'I'm just about
to have coffee. Would you like some?'

It was, she knew, the flimsiest of excuses and she could
see that the young woman also knew it. A fleeting look of

anger had been replaced by her usual impassivity. 'That's kind of you, Miss Hayward, but I've already had some. Peggy brought me a cup.'

Dilys held on to her smile. 'Fine.' She paused. 'You look very busy.'

'Yes, I have a—treatise to write.' Her tone made it clear further questions would be unwelcome. 'Seb hasn't been disturbing you, has he?'

'No, but I think he's awake. The pram's rocking.'

'He's quite happy lying there. I'll take him out as usual this afternoon.'

Dilys could think of no possible way of extending this awkward conversation. She had been snooping, and Sarah Baines knew it. All she could do was retire as gracefully as possible.

'Well, I'll leave you to your treatise, then,' she said brightly, and closed the door behind her.

Not a good move, she reflected as she returned downstairs. She had betrayed her curiosity and not unnaturally it was resented. What *was* it about that young woman that unsettled her? Outwardly she was polite and unassuming, and Susie thought highly of her. There was no doubt she was devoted to the baby; that morning Dilys had come upon them as Sarah was carrying him to his pram, surprising on her face an expression of almost maternal love which quickly neutralized at Dilys's approach. So why on earth should being in the same room with the girl raise the hairs on the back of her neck?

She resolved to harness her too-vivid imagination into more profitable channels and, regaining her study, sat down purposefully at her desk.

It was mid-afternoon before Webb had a chance to contact Nina, and considering it was she who'd requested a meeting, he was surprised by her air of diffidence as she entered his office.

He leant back in his chair, surveying her with interest. 'Well, Nina, how did it go?'

She wasn't quite meeting his eye. 'Fine, sir. All very pleasant and innocuous. I only looked in this morning to say I don't think it's worth continuing the investigation.'

He frowned. 'What about all those allegations of brain-washing and subliminal indoctrination?'

She gave a nervous laugh. 'A result of heightened imagin-ation, I'm afraid. I was looking for something suspicious and convinced myself I'd found it. But now I've had more time with them it's clear I was over-reacting, as I should have realized when I played back the speeches. There was nothing dangerous or threatening in them. In fact, it's a long time since I've met such a pleasant, friendly bunch of people.'

Webb said forcefully, 'Nina, they're fanatics, *that's* what makes them dangerous. Fanaticism is an unstable qual-ity—you never know what's going to trigger it off, and once that happens everything else goes out of the window.'

He waited for her comment but she remained silent. 'Sit down, then, and tell me what happened.'

She hesitated and he said again, more firmly, 'Sit down.' She perforce sat in the chair opposite him, clasping her hands in her lap. Across the room, Alan Crombie had looked up from his papers.

'Now,' Webb continued, 'you arrived at the house and then what?'

'I was greeted like a long-lost friend.'

'They tried to force drinks on you?'

'I was offered something, yes.'

'Did you accept it?' Webb feared this might be behind her change of attitude.

'No. At least,' she amended, 'not then. I did at the end of the meeting.'

'What changed your mind?'

She smiled slightly, remembering that nonsense about pomegranate seeds. She'd let her mother's fears make her paranoid! 'It seemed ridiculous—and rude—to keep refusing.'

'So what happened?'

'We watched another short film and then split into groups for discussion. It was fascinating.'

'The film was this Bellringer again?'

'Yes.'

'And what did he say this time?'

Nina said reluctantly, 'He was telling us about the new cities they're building, up in mountains all over the world. To be safe from the Flood.'

'He places a lot of faith in weather forecasts,' Webb said, watching her closely. She didn't smile. 'And are the animals going to be led up there, two by two?'

'No,' she answered seriously, 'they're not in danger. The Flood will be man's punishment—animals have done no wrong. In fact, they've been sinned against.'

'So they'll miraculously survive—sprout water-wings or something?'

They'd been warned to expect ridicule. 'I don't know,' she said.

Webb changed tack. 'All this building work must be costing them a packet?'

'Yes, they're continually trying to raise funds. Every member of the Movement' (Webb registered she no longer referred to it as a cult) 'pledges a tithe and there are fees for courses and instruction, sometimes costing hundreds of pounds. Also, to secure a place in Salvation City, everyone has to make regular contributions towards their own home there. If they can't keep up the payments, they lose their place.'

Something in the quality of Webb's silence penetrated Nina's understanding. Her tone changed, became more flippant, as she finished, 'Anyway, that's the gist of it.'

'Anything else?'

'Well, there were warnings not to expect anyone outside the Movement to understand.'

'And do you?' Webb asked quietly.

'Sir, you asked me to look into it and I'm simply repeating what happened. I thought that was what you wanted.'

'Yes, it was. Thank you. But you felt they were genuine?'

'Oh, no doubt about it. They passionately believe every word they say. But there's no pressure on anyone else—they keep stressing that. Anyone can drop out of instruction at any stage they want to. Honestly, sir, I think you've been worrying unnecessarily.'

Webb said carefully, 'You're probably right. That's that, then. Thanks for all the research, Nina. There's no need for you to go again.'

'Thank you, sir.'

He hesitated. 'In fact, it would be better all round if you didn't. The more you go, the more likely you are to be rumbled, and we don't know how they'd react to that.'

'No, sir.'

'That's understood, then? End of investigation?'

'Yes, sir.'

He nodded and she left the room. Crombie let out his breath in a low whistle.

'What the hell do you make of that?'

'I don't like it, Alan, but we'll have to find some other way of keeping an eye on them. I don't want Nina dabbling in it any more. She said earlier that that insidious stuff can get to anybody and if we're not careful we'll have *her* floating off to Salvation City or whatever it calls itself.'

'It never ceases to amaze me how gullible people are,' Crombie said, and returned to his papers.

But it was a minute or two before Webb was able to switch his mind back to the murder case. A niggling sense of unease persisted, and he found himself wishing he'd never agreed to Nina going along to that place. Thank God he'd been able to call a halt before it had gone too far.

Back in her cubby-hole of an office, Nina sat down at her desk. Well, she'd done what was required of her and the official part of it was over, thank goodness. She'd felt increasingly uncomfortable last night, knowing she was spying on them, betraying their friendship, and it had been a profound relief when she'd played the tape back at home and it had proved as innocent as before. She had discharged her duty and was now free to do as she wished.

And she wished—very much—to go back. There was so much more she wanted to know. Brad Lübekker had singled her out last night and they'd had a long talk about the growth of the Movement and the urgency in achieving its aims. What was more, he'd told her Captain Bellringer would be in London next week and wondered if she'd like to meet him. The thought of it made her weak. To meet in person that wonderful man who had so much strength of vision that he was able, single-handed, to hold out the hope of salvation. She felt confusedly that her whole life had been moving towards such a meeting.

And then, of course, there was Daniel—Daniel, who had been so proud for her at the attention the Elder was paying her, who had taken her hand as he walked with her to the door after the meeting. She smiled softly to herself. Sorry and all that, sir, but she was going back all right. Tonight.

CHAPTER 8

Hannah said slowly, 'I don't quite understand what you're saying, Matron.'

The woman in front of her flushed. 'To be honest, Miss James, I'm not sure I do myself. I just felt you should know.'

Hannah gazed at her thoughtfully. Janet Rimmer had been matron of Brontë House for the past four years. She was an efficient, sensible woman, not, Hannah would have said, over-endowed with imagination—but who wanted that in a matron?

'When exactly was this?'

'During the lunch break, when they should have been over at the school anyway. I was going down for lunch and heard this voice as I passed Marina Chase's room. That's why I stopped.'

'And you say it was a man's voice?'

'That's right. Of course, I realized at once it was either a tape or the radio, but there was something about it which caught my attention and I—I stopped to listen.'

Her flush deepened. 'Miss James, this sounds ridiculous, but it really was most disturbing. I couldn't have moved if I'd wanted to. It was all so plausible, yet so *wrong*.'

'But—was it pornographic? Is that what you mean?'

'No, no, nothing like that. In fact it was pseudo-religious, but *subversive*—really quite frightening. All about the end of the world, that Satan is everywhere and people are basically evil.'

'The dogma of original sin, subversive?' Hannah queried with raised eyebrow.

Janet Rimmer said stiffly, 'Perhaps I'm wasting your time.'

Hannah put out an impulsive hand. 'No, please, I was being flippant. I'm very grateful you told me. Did you speak to Miss Anthony?'

The house-mistress was also a down-to-earth woman.

'I went to her first, but she thought I could perhaps describe the undercurrents better, having heard them for myself. Not that I seem to be making a very good job of it. It was *nasty*, Miss James—that's really all I can say.'

'You didn't go in and tackle Marina about it?'

'No, to be honest I felt out of my depth. And she wasn't alone. When the tape ended, I heard her say, "Turn it over, Steph."'

The matron looked down at her clasped hands. 'You heard she and Stephanie came back from *exeat* as vegetarians? I was wondering if there was any connection, if it was something that happened during the weekend.'

Of course! The publicity sheet David had shown her, for a meeting to be held by—what had he called them? The Revvies? Stephanie and Marina were home that night—possibly at a loose end. Had they gone along out of curiosity? And if so, what had happened to them?

Seeing the woman's troubled eyes on her, Hannah said

slowly, 'I believe there was a meeting last Friday of this new cult people are talking about. Perhaps the girls went along.'

Miss Rimmer's face cleared. 'That would certainly explain it. But what were their parents thinking of, letting them go to something like that?'

'It's my bet their parents knew nothing about it.' Hannah's opinion was not high of either the Frenches or the Chases regarding their respective daughters. As long as the girls were out of the way and not making nuisances of themselves, they were left to their own devices. That much she had gleaned over the years, both from comments by the girls themselves and from what she had noted on Parents' Evenings. But she couldn't say as much to Matron.

'I think I'd better have a word with them,' she said.

'I hope it won't be necessary to reveal my part in this. I shouldn't like them to think I listen at doors—it's something I've always despised.'

'No names will be mentioned,' Hannah assured her. 'Thank you, Matron. If this does stem from last Friday, at least we can nip it in the bud before it gets a hold on them.'

Mattie Hendrix sat bolt upright on her chair. They were in the meeting room at Victoria Drive and it was like a tribunal, she thought fearfully. Facing her across the table was Prelate Lübekker, with Sarah—naturally—at his side, and Adam and Daniel at either end.

Had Nina been present she would scarcely have recognized the attractive, smiling man who had devoted so much time to her the previous evening. Now the craggy face was like granite, the eyes splinters of glass.

'You do realize, Sister Matilda,' he said in his slow, American drawl, 'that this is a serious matter?'

Mattie moistened her lips. 'Yes, sir.'

'There are thousands of people desperate for a place in Salvation City. In all fairness, we can't keep yours indefinitely if you fall behind with your payments.'

'But I put every penny I can spare into the fund, Prelate,'

she protested. 'The trouble was that the last course was more expensive than I'd budgeted for, and Sarah insisted it was compulsory.'

'She was correct. If you don't keep up with the courses, how will you learn enough to instruct others?'

He templed his fingers and looked at her over the top of them. 'Which brings me to another point. I see your enrolment record's disappointingly low.'

'Two girls from my school were here on Friday,' she said quickly.

'Coincidentally, I believe. Have you spoken to them since, made sure they had leaflets and cassettes?'

'No, sir.' Another black mark, she thought despairingly.

'Then it's fortunate Brother Terry supplied them, isn't it?'

So he'd known of her shortcomings all along.

'Can you explain why you yourself didn't do what was necessary?'

'I—I find it hard to speak of my faith.'

'So do we all, at times, but if no one made the effort, where would the Movement be? You're aware of the urgency. Time moves remorselessly on.' He studied her with his cold, cold eyes. 'How is your gospel progressing?'

She lied desperately. 'Quite well, thank you, Prelate.' If only she'd more *time*! But he'd just warned her it was running out, for all of them.

'Very well, that's all for the moment. But this has to be your final warning, Sister. Either you keep up your payments or you forfeit your place—and you know what the consequences of that would be.'

He nodded in dismissal and she escaped from the room and stumbled down the corridor to the kitchen. Lucy and Liz were finishing their tea and Lucy rose with a smile to fetch another mug. Mattie sank into a chair and put her head in her shaking hands.

'As bad as that?' Lucy said sympathetically. 'Here, drink this. Nothing like tea when you're down.'

'I don't know what to do,' Mattie said simply. She was

aware that she shouldn't discuss it with them; the hierarchy was strictly maintained and Gospellers such as herself did not confide in the lower level of Seekers.

'Money, is it?' Liz said shrewdly.

Mattie nodded, clasping her thin hands round the mug as though to draw warmth from it. 'But I haven't enrolled anyone for months either, and by the time I've corrected classwork every night I'm too tired to work on my gospel. I'm a failure, that's all there is to it. That's what the Prelate was really saying.'

'Nonsense!' said Liz robustly. 'You're doing your best, anyone can see that.'

'But it's not good enough,' Mattie insisted tremulously. 'This was my final warning. If I can't keep up the payments, I lose my stake in Salvation City.'

The girls stared at her in horror. It was obviously worse than they'd realized.

'Then concentrate on your gospel,' Liz advised after a moment. 'If the Elders think it has divine inspiration, they'll waive part of your fee. It's happened before.'

Mattie gave her a wan smile. 'I'll try to, but inspiration, divine or otherwise, is thin on the ground at the moment. Thanks for the tea and sympathy. I'd better be going— I've a pile of work to get through.'

'Why not do it here and stay on for supper? Daniel's bringing a guest—Nina—do you know her? Small and dark; she was here last night. I think he's rather smitten!'

A free meal was tempting in itself, let alone the sense of belonging, of being with friends. But the Prelate would also be there and she'd had enough of his company. 'Thanks all the same, but I'd better not. Another time, perhaps.' And pushing back her chair she gave a tug to her faded cardigan and hurried out of the room.

Mr Ray of the wine importers had identified the body and was now on his way back to London. Philip Kershaw had not made any telephone calls from his room during his brief occupancy, nor had anyone phoned the hotel inquiring for him. A blank all round.

So when, wondered Webb, had he arranged to meet the couple for whom he'd been waiting when Christina French saw him? From London, anticipating booking in at the King's Head? If so, it was not from his hotel; he'd phoned only the solicitors from there. Why on earth, Webb thought in exasperation, hadn't he made both appointments at the same time?

Abruptly he pulled the phone towards him and dialled the estate agents. He wanted a look at the Kershaw house; no doubt the electricity was off but he'd still about an hour of daylight, which should do him.

Calder's Close was a cul-de-sac of large Victorian houses off Westgate. They all looked fusty and out of date to Jackson, an impression emphasized by the gradually darkening day. The estate agents had been keen to accompany them, but the Governor wasn't having any of that and they'd had to give in. Lord knows what he hoped to find here.

Webb was striding ahead of him up the overgrown path and inserting the key in the door. It swung open, and they stepped over a pile of free newspapers and junk mail into the hallway.

Philip Kershaw had been here on Monday, either before or after his appointment with Soames. Why had he come? To collect some possessions of his own which had lain here all these years? Or to go through his mother's things and pack up what was personal? In either case, what had he done with them? They were not in his room at the King's Head.

An old-fashioned phone stood on a small oak table and Webb lifted it and listened for a moment. Dead. So he hadn't rung from here, either.

The progress through the large, silent rooms was oddly depressing. Jackson had brought a torch with him and directed its beam as Webb systematically opened cupboards and drawers, flicked through their contents and closed them again. There was nothing of interest. If there had been, Philip Kershaw must have removed it. It occurred to Webb that he didn't know what the old lady had died of. He must remember to ask. God, he wished they could track down Soames. There were all kinds of questions he could answer.

Following the torch beam, they went up the creaking staircase, groping their way on to the landing which the closed bedroom doors rendered almost dark.

'You take the left side, I'll do the right,' Webb instructed. 'And we'd better get a move on or we'll be in danger of breaking a leg going back down those stairs. I'll take the torch—give me a call if you need it.'

The first door he came to was probably Miss Preston's room. The bed was stripped, the dressing-table bare. He wondered idly what she'd do with her windfall.

'Guv!' Jackson's voice rang through the gloom, startling him. 'Come and have a dekko!'

Webb hurried across the dark landing.

'What do you make of this?'

Jackson was standing by the window in the last of the light, holding something in his hands. Webb joined him and saw it was an exquisite ivory carving of a Noah's ark, some eight inches long and six high.

'And there's all the animals lined up and all,' Jackson added, nodding to the fireplace behind Webb.

He turned sharply, peering through the gloom at the procession marching along the mantelpiece—miniature giraffes with delicate necks, elephants, crocodiles, tigers and many more, all neatly paired with their own kind.

'Odd sort of thing for an old lady to have, isn't it?'

'Yes, Ken,' Webb said slowly, 'a very odd thing.'

Coincidence? It must be, yet Webb wasn't sure he believed in coincidence.

'It's probably valuable,' he said. 'We'd better take it for safekeeping—I'll let young Soames know in the morning.' He opened the wardrobe door and shone the torch inside.

'There's a box of tissue paper in here. Wrap it all up, Ken. Carefully, now. Those legs and trunks are delicate.'

'Reckon the little French granddaughter'd like this,' Jackson commented, as he spread the paper on the bed and began his task. 'I'm surprised Mr Kershaw didn't take it for her.'

'It's hardly a toy, Ken.' But Webb, too, was surprised the Ark had been left behind. They'd found no jewellery or other valuables in the house, though circles on dusty surfaces downstairs indicated where ornaments might have stood. Perhaps Kershaw already had as much as he could carry—he'd not had a car, after all. He might have intended to return for the Ark later, but the queries that were exercising Webb would not have troubled him. As far as he was concerned, it would have been simply another of his mother's belongings.

'Hurry up, Ken,' Webb said suddenly, 'this place is starting to give me the willies.'

As soon as he reached his flat, Webb took the large bundle of tissue paper through to the living-room and laid it carefully on the wide surface of his desk. Then he poured himself a drink and lit the gas fire, briefly holding out his hands to the glow. It had been cold in the empty old house and he was still chilled.

Taking his glass with him, he went over to the desk, sat down on the chair in front of it and carefully began to unwrap the tissue paper. By the time the doorbell sounded, the Ark stood in pride of place and some ten sets of animals were laid out in front of it.

Hannah was waiting outside. 'There's a pleasant surprise!' he said, kissing her. 'Come in—I've something to show you.'

'And I've something to tell you.'

She walked ahead of him into the living-room and he heard her exclamation of surprise. 'What an exquisite thing, David! Where did you find that?'

'In the house of an old lady who died recently.'

'You mean you've bought it?'

'No, but it's too valuable to be left in the empty house.'

She took the drink he handed her. 'And what were you doing there? Had the old lady met a nasty end?'

'Not as far as I know.' He paused. 'But her son had.'

'Explain,' Hannah instructed, sipping her drink.

'The body at the King's Head. You might have read about it.'

'I saw something in the paper.'

'Well, while I've been looking into it—and it's complicated enough in all conscience—Nina Petrie, as I told you, has been sussing out the Revelationists. Two entirely separate investigations. Then, out of the blue, I come across this.'

'And you think there's a connection?'

'It's possible, wouldn't you say?'

'Any luck with Nina's sleuthing?'

'I've called a halt to it,' Webb said shortly.

She looked at him sharply. 'Why?'

'Partly at her recommendation and partly because of her change of attitude. She's done a complete about-turn—can't speak highly enough of them.'

'I don't think I like the sound of that.'

'Nor did I.'

'David, it's because of the cult that I called.' She opened her handbag and extracted a cassette. 'At least, I assume this is their work. Play it and see what you think. I confiscated it from two fifth-form girls.'

Thus it was that Webb was able to hear for himself the mesmeric voice of Noah Bellringer which Nina had struggled to describe for him, and the message it imparted was honeyed poison.

This version was aimed at young people, warning them to trust no one, since everyone outside the movement was evil and would try to discredit the Revelationists. Parents and teachers in particular were liable to spread false stories, and must be treated with suspicion.

'Remember,' the persuasive voice emphasized, 'Satan

has always tried to harm those who serve the Lord. Didn't our Lord himself say, He that is not with me is against me? You will meet scorn, ridicule and abuse on all sides but I say to you, Be strong! Trust only in the Lord and his servant Noah Bellringer and together we shall survive.'

The voice faded and after a minute there was a small click as the machine switched itself off.

'Strong stuff,' Webb commented. 'I'd like someone to have a look at that; I'm pretty sure it contains subliminal material, probably in the background music.' He looked at Hannah's grave face. 'Did you speak to the girls about it?'

'Yes, separately.'

'And what did they say?'

'Very little. I felt I wasn't getting through to them at all. Unfortunately, they're ideal targets for the Revvies; their respective parents are too caught up in their own affairs— business interests in one case, marital difficulties in the other—to pay them much attention.'

'So what will you do?'

'I've arranged to see their parents—I've no intention of taking sole responsibility for this. Anyway, if the girls *did* go to that meeting—which so far they haven't admitted— it was while they were under their parents' jurisdiction. Of course you can take the cassette, but not till after I've played it to them.'

She paused. 'I wonder if DI Petrie was subjected to some- thing like that.'

'I hope not. I should never have let her get involved in the first place; she's just the sort they cotton on to—youngish, divorced, probably lonely. I'll have an eye kept on them, but at least Nina's safely out of it.'

At the precise moment of Webb's comforting reflection, Nina herself was seated in the kitchen at Victoria Drive, a feeling of excitement pumping through her. There were ten of them round the table. Sarah and Mattie weren't there but she'd met Ruth and Annabel, whom she'd seen at the meeting handing round coffee cups. They were all so friendly and welcoming; it was obvious she'd been accepted, as Daniel's friend and almost certainly as a potential member of the Movement.

'You join as an Initiate,' Brad Lübekker was saying in answer to her question, 'and progress to Seeker, like the young people here.' His glance took in Liz, Lucy, and the boys who'd been talking to the schoolgirls on her first visit, now identified as Terry and Vince.

'And then what?' she asked.

Brad smiled. 'I can see there'll be no holding you! Gospeller comes next, but you need to take a four-week course to prepare for it.'

He refilled her glass with apple juice. 'You see, as a Gospeller you're required to write your own testament, or gospel, setting out your personal faith and experience of God. At the millennium, a selection of the most inspiring will be bound together to form a third and Final Testament.'

He glanced at her, pleased at her interest. 'We all have knowledge of God, Nina, but only a fraction is revealed to each one of us. By pooling our spiritual knowledge, we aim to complete the jigsaw of God's design and purpose for us.

'As you'll appreciate, people remain as Gospeller for several years, taking further courses during that time to assist their work. Daniel and Adam here are Gospellers, as are Sarah and Matilda, whom I believe you've also met.'

'And after Gospeller comes Pastor,' Adam put in, 'and then, right at the top, the Elders of the Movement, Prelates—like Brad—and High Priests.'

'And you say the Movement is world-wide?'

'Virtually, yes, but we're working against the clock. We must save as many as we can before the waters start to rise.'

Nina shuddered at the suddenly serious note in his voice, which dispelled the warm cosiness of their circle.

'Let us pray,' he added, 'that none of us will be found wanting in the task that lies ahead.'

Unselfconsciously, they bowed their heads and Nina,

listening to the words which poured so passionately from the Prelate, wondered how she could ever have doubted such a sincere and devout group of people.

Then it was time for her to go, and after she'd made her farewells, Daniel walked with her along the corridor to the front door. 'It's good to have you with us, Nina,' he said softly. 'I knew from the first that you were meant to join us.'

'Did you?' She looked up at him, and he suddenly bent and kissed her mouth. Her response was immediate but she held it down, fearful of the consequences of too swift a commitment. He was, after all, the first man to attract her since Ross had left. It was essential to remain in control.

'Good night, Daniel,' she said and, without looking back, ran down the steps and through the gate. Her mother, she knew, would be anxiously waiting. What was she going to tell her this time?

When Christina had arrived home that evening, there was a message from the school on the answerphone. Miss James would be grateful if Mr and Mrs French would call to see her at three o'clock the following afternoon, to discuss a problem that had arisen.

'A bit high-handed, isn't it?' Christina said over supper. 'We're busy people, after all; we can't drop everything the minute she lifts a finger.'

'That's hardly fair, darling. She's never sent for us before—there must be a good reason.'

Edward had a high opinion of Miss James. In fact, he was more comfortable with her than with Miss Rutherford who, though admittedly the possessor of a double first, nevertheless struck him as woolly-headed, flapping around as she did, spraying hairpins in all directions. Miss James was quite different, sensible and easy to talk to and an attractive woman into the bargain, with that heavy, honey-coloured hair.

'I don't see why it couldn't have waited till Parents' Evening,' Christina retorted.

Edward was struck by a disturbing thought. 'I wonder if Stephie's been playing up? She was behaving oddly last weekend—I told you—what with that vegetarian nonsense and throwing away all her make-up.'

Christina realized uncomfortably that she hadn't given a thought either to her daughter or her behaviour since the night Edward mentioned it. She made no further comment, but when the meal was over, went up to Stephanie's room.

As soon as she entered it she was aware of something different, something which, though she couldn't at first put her finger on it, disquieted her. Then she saw that the pictures of pop stars which normally decorated the walls had been removed and in their place a solitary piece of crumpled paper was stuck up with Blu-tack. Moving nearer, she made out the smudged outline of a triangle with a semi-circle behind it.

For a moment she stared at it, trying to make sense of it, then, baffled, turned away and her eyes fell on the wastepaper basket. As Edward had said, it was full of the jumbled contents of Stephie's make-up drawer—expensive and almost new lipsticks, the bottle of scent which had been her birthday present, eyeshadows, blusher and hair ribbons.

Instead of its normal clutter, the dressing-table was bare except for a small, empty jeweller's box. Christina recognized it as having contained the gold cross and chain which Stephie had been given by her godmother at her confirmation. At the time she'd worn it constantly, though, Christina suspected, more as ornament than emblem, being the only form of jewellery permitted by the school.

But that was years ago and she couldn't remember when she'd last seen it. So where was the cross now? Had it been lost, given away? Or had Stephie started wearing it again? And if so, did this tie in with the discarded make-up, the rejection of meat?

Sometimes girls went through a religious phase in their teens, Christina thought. That's probably all it was, though it must have been a sudden and extreme conversion. Was this what Miss James wanted to speak to them about?

Looking round the bare walls, Christina had an irrational desire to see again the grinning face of Jason Donovan. She gave an involuntary little shiver and went hurriedly out of the room, closing the door carefully behind her.

CHAPTER 9

'Ken? Bring the car round, will you? I want to see Miss Preston again.'

'Right, Guv.' Jackson raised his eyebrows. He couldn't imagine what more the housekeeper could tell them, but no doubt Spiderman knew what he was doing.

'Something else come up, has it? he asked, as they drove along Carrington Street.

'It's about the Ark,' Webb said briefly.

'The Noah's Ark? That we found in the house?'

'The very same. You said yourself it was an odd thing for an old lady to have. I want to know how long she's had it and where it came from.'

Light began to dawn. 'You think she might have been in touch with that lot the DI was looking into?'

'That, my lad, is what I intend to find out.'

This time it was the owner of the bungalow who opened the door.

'If you're looking for my sister she's in the back garden,' she told them. 'You can go round the side of the house.'

Webb thanked her and in single file they made their way through the narrow side-gate. The back garden was ablaze with multicoloured chrysanthemums and dahlias and edged with bright-berried shrubs. In the centre of a paved area stood an old-fashioned sundial, and at the far end Webb could see a small pond with an artificial heron standing beside it. The effect was of a stately home garden in miniature, charming, but over-fussy for his taste.

Miss Preston, clad in cord trousers, sweater and boots,

turned in surprise at their approach. 'Good morning, Chief Inspector. I wasn't expecting another visit!'

'No, ma'am, nor was I, but there are a few more questions, I'm afraid.'

'Then let's sit on the bench in the sunshine,' she suggested, leading the way to an old garden seat under an apple tree. 'Now,' as they all settled themselves, 'fire away!'

'First, I forgot to ask you what Mrs Kershaw died of?'

'Oh, it was her heart—she'd been on tablets for years. She didn't have an attack, as far as we know, just went peacefully in her sleep.'

'I see.' It seemed innocuous enough but he'd check with her GP. 'The other thing I was wondering was whether she had any friends who came to visit her?'

'Well, if you could call them friends. There were some young people who kept popping round. I thought she'd get tired of them for ever looking in, but she was always glad to see them. I suppose she'd missed the company of young people over the years.'

'Were they children of friends?' Webb asked, though he thought he knew the answer.

'Oh no, nothing like that. The girl called one day collecting for charity, and while I was looking in my purse, she remarked on an old tree that was leaning over the path. She said it looked dangerous, and she had a friend who'd be willing to cut it down for us if we liked.

'I went to ask Mrs Kershaw, and she told me to take the girl in to see her. Lucy, her name was. So it was all arranged and at the weekend a young man came round, and I must say he made a very good job of it. Didn't seem to want any money for it, either. In the end he suggested Mrs Kershaw made a donation to the same charity, which she did.

'And it went on from there. He and another lad started doing all sorts of jobs around the house—putting new washers on taps, changing plugs, clearing out gutters. The girls helped out, too, Lucy and a friend of hers—and gradually they started dropping in for tea or to spend the evening. Mrs Kershaw seemed charmed with them.

'I was suspicious for a while, wondering if they were planning to burgle the house once they knew the layout. Nor did I like leaving the old lady alone with them, and even though I wasn't needed, I made excuses for staying in the house. But I soon realized that I'd wronged them. They seemed genuinely fond of her and she of them. And they all came to her funeral, which is more than most people did.'

'Did you ever join them for tea?'

'No; once I'd left it ready, the afternoon was my own. In fact, I had more free time over the last few months than during all the years I was with her.'

'What were the others called?'

'There was Ruth and Vince, and the other young man was Terry, I think. Oh, and Liz, but she only came once or twice. I never heard any surnames.'

'What did you think of them? Did you like them?'

Miss Preston hesitated, brushing a leaf off her cord trousers. 'There was nothing about them to *dis*like.'

'That doesn't answer my question.'

She smiled. 'I realize that, but I can't really give a straight answer. They were always friendly and charming and yet—this sounds ridiculous—I felt they were too good to be true. And I suppose I resented them coming so often, which, again, was stupid, because it meant I had time to myself.'

'You felt they were trying to ingratiate themselves?'

'Yes, that's it exactly! That's just what I felt.'

'Did they ever bring her presents?'

Miss Preston looked surprised. 'Presents? I don't think so.'

'Miss Preston, Sergeant Jackson and I went round to the house last evening and we found an elaborately carved Noah's Ark complete with animals. Quite a work of art.'

'Oh—the Ark, yes.'

'Can you tell us about it? Had Mrs Kershaw had it long?'

'No, only a few weeks, but it wasn't from the young

people, that was from someone else. I'd forgotten about him.'

'And who was he?'

'I don't know his name—that was the only time I saw him. He came to the house one evening a week or two before she died. He must have brought it, because I saw it for the first time after he'd gone.'

'Had he any connection with the others?'

'I shouldn't think so—he was quite a bit older. But Mrs Kershaw never discussed any of them with me—she was a very private person. She didn't say who the man was or why he'd called, and it wasn't my place to ask.'

'Did she make any comment on the Ark?'

'Not in so many words, but she was obsessed with it— wouldn't let it out of her sight. I had to bring it downstairs every morning and take it back up again at night. She couldn't manage it herself, because of her stick. And often when I came into the room she was just sitting staring at it. To be honest, it gave me the creeps.'

'One last question, Miss Preston. What charity was the girl collecting for?'

'Oh, something to do with the Third World—I forget the name.'

In all probability, Webb reflected grimly, the 'third world' referred to was not the one usually associated with the phrase. He watched a group of blackbirds splashing in the pond, his mind revolving round what he'd just heard. Lucy and Ruth, Vince and Terry, Liz. Would those names mean anything to Nina? He was damn sure they would.

'Hannah?'

'Hello, Dilys! How are you?'

'Decidedly twitchy, my dear.'

'Oh, how so? The baby proving a distraction after all?'

'Not in himself, I have to say. It's probably just me. Hannah, I have a favour to ask. Could you possibly call round today or tomorrow? For tea, perhaps, or drinks if you prefer?'

'Today's out, I'm afraid. I'm seeing some parents this afternoon and there's a meeting after school.'

'Tomorrow, then? Please?'

'You do sound edgy—what's wrong?'

Dilys lowered her voice till Hannah had to strain to hear it. 'It's this nanny, Hannah. There's something strange about her—really strange—and it worries me having her in the house.'

'But surely Susie was—'

'Yes, I know, I keep telling myself that.'

'You don't think—' horror crept into Hannah's voice— 'you don't think she'd do anything to the baby, do you?'

'No, I don't,' Dilys said positively. 'She dotes on him. That's her only saving grace, as far as I'm concerned.'

'But—'

'Look, I can't explain. I just want you to meet her and tell me what you think. You're a good judge of character; if you tell me I'm being barmy, I'll believe you and perhaps be able to get down to this blasted book again. Please, Hannah.'

'Of course, if you're as worried as that. Tomorrow, then, and tea would be lovely.'

'Fine. You don't know what a load that is off my mind.'

Hannah replaced the phone thoughtfully. Dilys had always had a hyperactive imagination—it was, after all, how she earned her living. But Hannah had never known her react so strongly to someone before. She would be quite interested to see this nanny for herself.

'Excuse me, Miss Hendrix—'

Mattie, alone in the classroom at the end of the morning's lessons, jumped and looked towards the door. Stephanie French and Marina Chase stood watching her hesitantly and her heart plummeted. She'd been expecting this for the last week.

'Yes?'

'We wondered if you could help us. Miss James has

confiscated our cassettes and pamphlets—we thought you ought to know.'

'Cassettes?' Mattie echoed weakly, to gain time.

'Yes, that we were given last week. She found out about them somehow, and sent for us to ask what they were all about.'

This was worse than Mattie had expected and her heart set up a loud, frightened hammering. 'What did you tell her?'

'Nothing.' It was said with a touch of defiance.

'Did you—mention my having been at the meeting?'

'No.'

She felt a wave of relief. Would she have denied her beliefs if Miss James had confronted her with them? Oh, if only she had the strength that was needed to be a Gospeller!

No wonder the Prelate had taken her to task last night. She had, he implied, been handed these two young minds on a plate—an ideal opportunity to draw them in. And what had she done? Nothing! Even now, when they'd come to her for help, she was wavering hopelessly.

She said, 'What do you want me to do?'

The girls looked at each other as though puzzled by her indecisiveness, as well they might be.

'Could you get us some more? We're supposed to play them every day.'

'Yes, I'll—I'll get you some.'

'Thank you.' They waited uncertainly for a moment longer, and when she remained silent, went together out of the room.

Mattie put her head down on the desk and wept. What a weak, spineless fool! She'd been given the perfect chance to talk to the girls, have a discussion with them—they were obviously hungry for knowledge. She even had papers and tapes of her own she could have lent them. And what had she done with this heaven-sent opportunity? Sat with her eyes fearfully on the door behind them, longing for them to leave before someone came along. What kind of disciple was she? A failed one, that much was obvious. A failed disciple with a failed life.

She lifted her head, fumbling for a handkerchief and trying to control herself sufficiently to go along to the dining-hall. The only thing that kept her going, she thought, was her love of teaching and at that, she knew, she excelled. It was small comfort, but it was all she had.

When Webb returned to Carrington Street, it was to find a message waiting for him. Roderick Soames and his wife had been located in Scotland, given the news of Kershaw's murder, and were flying home that evening. Thank God for that, he thought. He was counting on Soames for the answers to several outstanding queries.

He lifted the intercom on his desk. 'Nina, could you spare a moment?'

'I've got some names which I imagine are associated with your lot,' he greeted her as she came into his office. 'Lucy, Ruth, Vince, Terry, Liz. Mean anything to you?'

Nina said steadily, 'Yes, they're all Revelationists.'

He tilted his chair back, his eyes on her face. 'What are they like?'

'Very pleasant.'

'A little more than that, Inspector, if you please.'

'What do you want to know, sir? They're in their early to mid-twenties, I'd say. The boys help out at the Youth Club; Ruth's a doctor's receptionist; Lucy and Liz are unemployed.' She'd learned all that the previous evening. 'Why?' she added, when he remained silent.

'Just that they'd been sniffing round the mother of our murder victim.'

'Did she make a complaint?'

'Far from it. Gave them tea and had them round for the evening.'

Nina nodded, as though she'd have expected as much, which for some reason annoyed Webb.

'The housekeeper thought they were making a nuisance

of themselves,' he added shortly. 'All right, thank you. That's all.'

There was no need for the Governor to be so hostile to the group, Nina thought resentfully, forgetting it was she who'd originally implanted his suspicions. But they were warned to expect hostility and, to be fair to the DCI, there had been complaints that children were being alienated.

Momentarily, she thought of Alice and a quiver went through her. But she'd trust her with the Revelationists any day, of course she would. In fact, Daniel had already asked to meet her. The trouble would be trying to explain his presence to Mother.

When they arrived at the school that afternoon the Frenches were surprised, and not pleased, to find the Chases also waiting to see Miss James. Relations had been strained since Edward had come face to face with Gordon and his 'fancy woman', as he termed her, in Ashmartin a month or two back.

Not, he reflected now, that they had ever been friends. Put bluntly, the Chases were social climbers, and it was only the friendship of their daughters that had forced some kind of bond between them.

'Do you know what this is about, old man?' Gordon Chase asked with false heartiness. 'Smoking behind the bike sheds or something?'

'Oh, surely not!' his wife put in, flashing a nervous glance at Christina and regretting her own choice of outfit. How had she ever thought this dress suited her? And she did wish Gordon wouldn't force himself on Edward like that. Anyone could see he was gritting his teeth to remain civil. Oh God, *why* had they sent Marina to this snooty school? She always felt like a duck out of water here.

'Well, if she *does* smoke, old thing, she'll have got it from you.' Gordon had detected her disapproval and was stung by it. 'Regular old chimney these days!'

'It calms my nerves,' Diane snapped back, and turned quickly to Christina. 'It was so sweet of you to invite

Marina over last weekend, but we'd planned a family celebration. I hope you didn't mind?'

Christina smiled without replying. Since Marina had apparently spent the weekend with Stephie anyway, no celebration, family or otherwise, had been in evidence.

Their discomfort was ended by the school secretary coming for them, though Hannah was conscious of the residual friction as she greeted them.

The contrast between the two families could hardly have been more marked: Mr French tall, carelessly well-dressed and sure of himself; Mr Chase, florid-faced and slightly rumpled, with a defensive smile on his face. And the women might have belonged to different species, the one so elegant and *soignée*; the other with tightly permed hair and a skimpy dress that did nothing for her. But as Edward turned on the charm, he might have been surprised to know with which couple her main sympathies lay.

'Thank you so much for coming,' she began as they seated themselves. There was a tray on a side table and the secretary poured tea and handed it round before quietly leaving the room. Immediately, Diane's prime concern became how to balance the fragile cup and saucer without spilling the tea, and to eat silently the crisp biscuit which accompanied it.

'As you'll have gathered,' Hannah was continuing, 'something rather worrying has happened, but before I explain, I'd be grateful if you could tell me how the girls spent last weekend.'

Four startled pairs of eyes met hers and immediately dropped away. She waited politely. Edward French, naturally, was the first to recover.

'Stephanie went to a disco, didn't she, darling?'

To her annoyance, Christina felt herself flush. 'I believe so, yes.'

'You *believe*, Mrs French?'

'That's where she usually goes. I told her to be back by eleven and to phone if she wanted collecting.' Which, surely, was all that was required of her; but when Hannah didn't immediately speak, she added with a malicious glance at Diane, 'She was with Marina.'

'This was Friday evening?'

Christina nodded.

'And did you collect her?'

'No, she was home by ten-thirty.'

'Surely she made some comment about her evening?'

'No.' Impatient to make love, they'd simply bidden her good night and gone straight upstairs.

'And you didn't ask her?'

Belated guilt made Christina snappy. 'We don't interrogate our daughter, Miss James. If she volunteers anything, fine. Otherwise we don't pry.'

'With fifteen-year-old girls "prying", as you call it, can sometimes be very necessary. Last Friday might well have been one of those times. What about Saturday, then?'

Christina was beginning actively to dislike the woman. 'On Saturday I had to fly up to Scotland on business. I didn't get back till Monday, after Stephanie had returned to school. My husband, naturally, was at home.'

Hannah turned with raised eyebrow to Edward, who also looked uncomfortable. 'Actually, I was embroiled in a golf competition most of the weekend,' he admitted. 'Unfortunate in the circumstances, but there you are. That's how things work out sometimes.'

Hannah's voice was dangerously quiet. 'Did you have any contact with your daughter over the weekend, Mr French?'

'Of course I did,' Edward blustered. 'We had breakfast together both days, and I was home in time to run her back here on Sunday evening.' He paused. 'I even offered to cook her bacon and eggs, but she floored me by announcing she'd turned vegetarian.'

Hannah leaned forward. 'Was that on Saturday or Sunday?'

What the hell did it matter? 'Saturday, just after my wife left. I remember wishing she was there to deal with it.'

'So you've no idea how Stephanie spent either Saturday

or Sunday while you were—embroiled in the golf competition?'

He reddened and shook his head. Damn woman, showing
him up in front of the Chases. It was about time she started
lashing into them. Which· she proceeded to do.

'What about Marina, Mrs Chase? Was she with you all
weekend?'

Diane started at being addressed, and some biscuit
crumbs fell on the carpet. She tried to rub them in with
her shoe. 'Er, no, not all the time.'

'So what did *she* do on Friday evening?'

'She went to a meeting.' It was said with a triumphant
glance at Christina; at least *she'd* known where her daughter
was. 'I thought it was something the school had arranged,'
she added diplomatically, 'specially since Stephanie was
going.'

'Did she tell you about it afterwards?'

'Oh yes, she was full of it—very flushed and excited.'

'So what kind of a meeting was it?'

'A religious one. They met two nice boys there and were
going to see them the next day.'

'And did they?'

'Yes, she was out all day Saturday. I didn't worry; I
thought if the boys were religious, they must be all right.
When she came back, she told me she was going to stop
wearing make-up because it was a kind of deception, and
anyway, Terry said she didn't need it. And she didn't want
to eat meat or fish any more either.'

'I didn't know all this,' Gordon interrupted.

'That's because you weren't there,' his wife retorted.

'You mean they've gone *religious*?' Edward sounded
dazed.

'I think,' Hannah said, lifting a cassette player on to the
desk, 'it's time we listened to this.' She switched it on,
watching the four of them as they sat in stunned silence
while the tape played itself through.

Then Edward said in a strangled voice, 'Who the devil
was that?'

'Devil's right,' Gordon muttered.

'He's the leader of a New Age cult called the Revelation-ists. I believe it was their meeting the girls went to on Friday.'

'Where did you get the tape?' Christina demanded.

'From Marina, but Stephanie was with her. Someone overheard them playing it. They'd a sheaf of pamphlets in their lockers, containing more of the same.'

'But they don't *believe* it, surely?' Diane asked shakily.

'Mrs Chase, they're young, impressionable girls. I can think of many adults who'd be taken in by it.'

'But what can we *do*?'

'Hope we're in time to stop them getting too deeply involved. They're under constant supervision here, but I'd strongly advise you not to leave them to their own devices during the holidays, at least until this has had time to die down. I realize,' Hannah added, with an edge to her voice, 'that it might be inconvenient, but you now know the dangers they can be exposed to.'

She stood up and came round the desk to hand each of the men a small card. 'This is the telephone number of Cult Helpline, which was set up specifically for the families of those involved with these sects. They'll be able to advise you. In the meantime, the best thing you can do is surround your daughters with love and understanding, stress how much they mean to you, and hope they'll respond.'

They couldn't get out of her study quickly enough, Hannah noted ruefully, aware that the home-truths she'd hinted at had not been palatable. Not that she'd any sympathy with them—particularly the Frenches, whose cavalier attitude amounted to neglect.

Hannah sighed and glanced at her watch, saw that she had barely an hour before the staff meeting and settled down with some work.

As it happened, she'd not even that. Less than five minutes after the parents had left her, a quick tap on the door brought her secretary, white-faced, into the room.

'Miss James, I'm sorry to disturb you, but Miss Hendrix has been taken ill.'

Hannah exclaimed with concern, pushing back her chair. 'What happened? Where is she?'

'Matron's taken her to the sick-room. As to what happened, I'm not sure. She was in the middle of a class and just seemed to collapse.'

Lack of food, probably, Hannah thought as she hurried to the sick-room and pushed open the door. Miss Baxter, the school matron, was bending over the narrow bed on which Miss Hendrix sat with her face in her hands, sobbing hysterically.

The matron turned a worried face towards her. 'I've phoned for Dr Templeton, Miss James. I've no idea what's wrong but I think sedation is indicated.'

'Which class was she taking, do you know?'

'The Lower Sixth, in room thirty-one.'

Hannah nodded and, since she could do no more for the invalid at the moment, hurried away to see what she could learn.

The hum of apprehensive chattering reached her as she came up the stairs, stopping abruptly when she appeared in the doorway. The entire class rose to its feet. Hannah's eyes, flicking down the rows of anxious young faces, alighted on one of the prefects.

'Sit down, everyone. Caroline, will you tell me, please, what happened to Miss Hendrix?'

Caroline Dashwood remained standing. 'She was testing us on *Macbeth* quotations, Miss James—act, scene, characters—that kind of thing. We weren't doing too well and Miss Hendrix had to prompt us several times. Then she asked whether a certain passage came before or after Duncan was murdered, and we got that wrong, too. And suddenly her face just crumpled. She hurled the piece of chalk on to the floor and just collapsed over the desk, sobbing and crying. It was awful, Miss James. We didn't know what to do, so Roberta ran for Matron.'

'Did she say anything before she collapsed?'

Caroline's voice shook. 'I think she said, "Now I can't even teach any more!" That made it worse, as though it was our fault.' She added almost pleadingly, 'Is she feeling better now?'

'I'm afraid not. The best way you can help is to settle down quietly and revise the passages you fell down on. You owe her that, at least.'

Which was probably unfair, Hannah thought as she ran back down the stairs, but at least it should ensure silence in the classroom for the remainder of the lesson which, thank God, was the last of the afternoon.

By the time she regained the sick-room, John Templeton, who, as well as being the school doctor, was also Gwen's brother-in-law, was attending to Miss Hendrix. He turned to meet Hannah's anxious eyes.

'I'll come to your study, Miss James, when I've completed my examination.'

'Thank you, Doctor.'

Hannah returned perforce to her room. Oh Gwen, she thought despairingly, I do wish you were here!

'It's been a horrible day,' Hannah commented to Webb some hours later. 'I had both sets of parents in to hear the tape, which involved lambasting them for not keeping an eye on their daughters. They didn't take kindly to it, especially the Frenches. Then, to crown everything—'

'The Frenches?' Webb interrupted.

'That's right— Stephanie French is one of the girls we're concerned about.'

'Does her mother run an interior decorating business?'

'Yes, French Furnishings. Do you know her?'

'Oddly enough, it was she who was talking to our murder victim shortly before he was killed.'

'Really? It's not her week, is it?'

'Sorry, I interrupted you. Go on.'

'Well, no sooner had they left than a member of staff collapsed during class and had to be carted off to sick-bay. John Templeton says she's suffering from exhaustion brought on by malnutrition, which doesn't surprise me. Anyway, he's transferred her to the san and wants to keep an eye on her for a day or two.'

She held out her glass as Webb refilled it. 'And to round everything off, we had a staff meeting which was heavier going than usual and I'd a splitting headache by the end of it. You do realize this second drink is purely medicinal?'

'But of course.'

She smiled up at him. 'So having got all that off my chest, how did your day go?'

'Quite interesting. The Noah's Ark was given to Mrs Kershaw by an unknown gentleman during the last weeks of her life. I'm told she was obsessed with it, never letting it out of her sight. I reckon we all know what that means. And for good measure a gang of Revvies had been making themselves useful to her, doing odd jobs around the house and generally getting into her good books.'

'Converting her into the bargain?'

'Almost definitely.'

'Do they present all their converts with works of art?'

'Only, I should say, the most generous of them.'

'Aha! The will rears its ugly head!'

'Exactly. And thank God the errant solicitor is on his way home. I should know a good deal more by this time tomorrow.'

CHAPTER 10

Solicitors, lucky beggars, didn't work on Saturdays, so Soames was calling in at Carrington Street. Having pinned so much on his visit, Webb hoped it wouldn't be an anti-climax.

He arrived punctually at ten o'clock, a tall, broad-shouldered man in his fifties with black, thinning hair and horn-rimmed spectacles. He came into the room quickly, holding out his hand. 'Chief Inspector Webb? This is very bad news.'

Jackson, who had gone downstairs to meet him, sat down unobtrusively, his notebook at the ready.

'Yes, sir. I'm sorry to have interrupted your holiday.'

The solicitor brushed aside such a consideration and took the chair Webb indicated. 'I hadn't seen any reports of the case, naturally, or I should have come home sooner. Perhaps you could fill me in.'

Webb did so, swiftly and succinctly.

'So the poor chap must have died shortly after leaving me?'

Webb nodded. 'In the circumstances, anything you can tell me about his visit, what you discussed and so on could be of the greatest importance.'

'I'll tell you, willingly, though I can't see how it will help. It was all family business. As you might have heard, Mr Kershaw's mother, a longstanding client of ours, died a few weeks ago. Mr Kershaw lived in France, and this was the first opportunity we'd had to discuss her affairs.'

'And her will?' Webb prompted gently.

The solicitor looked slightly discomfited. 'Yes, indeed.'

'I believe Mrs Kershaw was a wealthy woman?'

'That's true, Chief Inspector.' The solicitor shifted awkwardly on his chair. 'I don't know if you've heard, but unfortunately she and her son had become estranged.'

'So I gather. Do you know why?'

'A gambling debt, I believe. Mrs Kershaw had frequently been called on to "bail him out", as it were, and eventually she put her foot down. Harsh words were said on both sides, and sadly they were never reconciled.'

'How long ago was this?'

'Must be ten years now. Tragic.'

'So she never saw her granddaughter?'

'Not even her daughter-in-law.'

'But,' Webb said gently, 'he would still expect to inherit his mother's estate? There was no one else, after all.'

Soames sighed. 'Yes, he did indeed. In fact, he was

counting on it to get him out of some financial difficulties.'

'What kind of figure are we talking about?'

'We shan't know exactly, of course, until the assets and liabilities are ascertained and the tax paid, but at a rough estimate the net estate after tax is likely to be in the order of £250,000.'

Webb whistled softly. 'And how much went to Mr Kershaw?'

'Not,' said the solicitor with deliberation, 'one penny piece.'

Webb stared at him. 'He wasn't mentioned at all?'

'No. There was a legacy to Miss Margaret Preston, who'd been her housekeeper-companion for some years. But the residuary beneficiary—' he broke off, cleared his throat, then finished in a rush, as though glad to get it over—'is the Church of the Final Revelation.'

There was a long silence. Then Soames said anxiously, 'I don't know if you've heard of it?'

'Oh, I've heard of it, all right.' No wonder they could afford to fork out an ivory Ark.

'I did try to dissuade her,' Soames went on. 'Tried very hard, in fact, but she was implacable. Her son was to receive nothing. "He'd get through the lot in six months," she said.' Soames sighed again. 'Pity he had to find out right at the end like that—much better to have gone without knowing.'

'Just a minute: are you saying Kershaw didn't know the terms of the will until he saw you?'

'That's right. It was stipulated that he must be told in person, together with a homily on the sins of gambling, which I won't bore you with.' He shook his head sadly. 'Talk about revenge from beyond the grave.'

'And what,' asked Webb with interest, 'was his reaction?'

'As you'd imagine. Disbelief, shock, a torrent of abuse about his mother. And, of course, he was determined to contest it. Undue influence, that kind of thing.'

'Would it have stood up in court?'

'Only if he could have proved the Church had come

between mother and son, which as we know was not the case. Before they came on the scene, she was planning to divide it between other charities.'

'So what was decided?'

'Well, as you'll appreciate, I was in an invidious position. We were, after all, acting for his mother, not him. All I could do was suggest he contact his own solicitors and see what they advised. It was a most uncomfortable half-hour, I can tell you, Chief Inspector.'

'Do you know who his solicitors were?'

'I'm afraid not. A London firm, I believe.'

Webb toyed with his pen, tapping first one end of it and then the other on the desk. 'Were you aware that he'd called at the house?'

'Yes, he arrived at my office with a bagful of ornaments and trinkets. Felt they should be in safekeeping, he said. Of course, at that point he thought they belonged to him.'

'Did he say how he was going to spend the rest of the day?'

Soames shook his head. 'For two pins he'd have gone straight back to France, but his seat was booked on a flight the following day. Pity he *didn't* go home, as things turned out.'

'You knew he was staying at the King's Head?'

'He didn't say so, but it was an obvious choice.'

'Did he mention contacting anyone else in Shillingham?'

'Not to me, but I doubt if he knew anyone; he'd not lived here for twenty years.'

'What time did he leave you?'

'About twelve-fifteen.'

The solicitor's office was barely five minutes' walk from the King's Head. Kershaw must have gone straight there— in need of a stiff drink, no doubt. But when had he arranged that fatal meeting?

'Presumably you informed the Revelationists of their windfall?'

'Naturally. And Miss Preston.'

'Well, thank you for your help, Mr Soames, and for

cutting short your holiday. I'll come back to you if I may, should any other queries arise.'

The solicitor nodded soberly and Jackson saw him downstairs.

'Quarter of a million smackeroos, Guv!' he commented on his return.

'A fair bit of pocket-money there,' Webb agreed.

'You'd think she'd have left the poor bloke *something*.'

'Yes; I'm not surprised he hit the roof.'

'So what do we do now?'

'I think, Ken, it's time we paid a visit to the Revvies.'

The address of the sect was on the piece of paper Nina had given him. It was Saturday morning—with luck someone would be home.

'While I think of it, Guv,' Jackson said as they walked round to the car, 'Vicky asked me to thank you for her birthday card. It was good of you to remember.'

'I keep a note of the dates in my diary. How's young Tim these days?' The Jacksons' youngest child, one of twins, was Webb's godson.

'Growing apace like the rest of them. Millie was saying you must come round to tea when this lot's cleared up.'

'Good of her,' Webb said noncommittally. Though fond of the Jackson brood, he was not at his ease with young children. Or children of any age, come to that, he reflected morosely—especially young girls who went waltzing off to join weird sects. He was glad that was Hannah's problem rather than his.

No. 5, Victoria Drive was of the same period as Mrs Kershaw's house, but in a different price bracket. It was nevertheless a handsome enough house, fitting in anonymously with its neighbours so that a casual glance gave no hint of the secrets it contained.

The door was opened by a dark man in an open-necked shirt and jeans. 'Good morning,' he said pleasantly.

'Good morning, sir. Shillingham CID—DCI Webb and Sergeant Jackson.'

Webb fancied the eyes became more guarded, though the smile remained in place. 'And how can we help you, Chief Inspector?'

'Perhaps we could have a word? It shouldn't take long.'

They were shown into a room on the right of the door. It was fitted as a study, with two desks, each bearing a word-processor and printer, two tables, three filing cabinets and a photocopier. Several thousand pounds' worth of equipment, Webb reckoned in a cursory glance.

Their host turned the chairs round and they sat facing each other in the centre of the room.

'If I could have your name, sir?'

'Sorry—Reed, Adam Reed.'

'And your position in the household?'

Reed smiled slightly. 'We don't have positions that you would recognize, Chief Inspector. But if you mean, am I the owner, no. The house belongs to the Church and there are at present eight tenants, of which I am one. If you've questions to ask, I suppose I'm as good as anyone.'

'We're looking into the death of Mr Philip Kershaw last Monday.'

'Oh yes, I read about it.'

'I believe your Church has been named as residuary beneficiary under his mother's will?'

'That's quite correct. A magnificent gift.'

'Did you know Mrs Kershaw, sir?'

'Not personally, no.'

'But several of your—household visited her on a number of occasions?'

'That's right. They were glad to do what they could for her.'

'Goodness reaping its own reward,' Webb commented drily.

'As you say.'

'Were you aware of her son's existence?'

Reed stood up. 'Look, if it's Mrs Kershaw you want to speak about, you'd do better with Lucy. She knew her quite well.'

Webb had been working round to that. 'Then by all means let us see Lucy.'

The girl who joined them was a little overweight, with a plain but pleasant face.

'They're asking about Mrs Kershaw, Luce,' Reed prompted, after introducing her.

Her smile faded. 'Oh yes, poor lady. We do miss her.'

Though no doubt the quarter-million would temper their grief, Webb thought caustically. 'Did she ever mention her son to you?'

'Only once, and from the way she spoke of him we thought he was dead.'

'What did she say?'

'That she wasn't used to young company since her son had gone. It was a terrific shock when we saw his name in the paper.'

'You'd no idea of the estrangement?'

'None whatever.'

Her guileless blue eyes met his, and he could only believe her. Unless she was an uncommonly good actress, which seemed unlikely, she was surely telling the truth.

'Did she mention that she intended leaving everything to the Church?'

'She hinted at it, yes. It seemed the answer to our prayers.'

And as yet, they didn't know the sum involved.

'But when you learned about her son, did you feel, perhaps, that you'd no right to the money?'

Lucy looked perplexed and turned to Reed, who came to her assistance. 'By the time we heard about him, he was dead as well. But in any case, the old lady could do as she chose with her own money and if, as you say, her son was estranged, it's not surprising she acted as she did.'

'He has a wife and child in France. Don't you think they have a claim?'

'That's not for us to say. We've done nothing illegal, Chief Inspector, and you really can't expect me to agree the money should go elsewhere. After all, we're in a unique position to use it wisely and well to the maximum benefit.'

'Doing what?' Webb challenged him.

'Saving souls from hell.' It was said quite matter-of-factly and Webb felt uncomfortable. He himself had an ambivalent relationship with the Almighty, invoking Him in moments of crisis and forgetting Him the rest of the time. Whereas however misguided these Revvies might be, there was no denying their faith was deep and unshakeable. Perhaps that was where their strength—and their menace—lay.

He was tempted to ask about their beliefs, but that wasn't what he was being paid for. As Nina had said, both Reed and the girl seemed harmless, but with that faith burning inside them there was no knowing what they were capable of when the need arose.

Nodding to Jackson, Webb got to his feet. 'Thank you for your time,' he said formally, and felt a certain relief when the outer door closed behind them.

They had driven out to the Chantock Hills, parked the car and set off to climb the nearest ridge. Alice was running happily ahead of them, stopping every now and then to pick wild flowers.

Suddenly, feeling the tug of her muscles as the climb steepened and the wind stinging her face, Nina felt a surge of intense happiness. The smell of warm grass, the racing clouds, Alice's long, windblown hair and—yes—Daniel at her side, had come together in an explosion of joy that made her want to sing aloud.

As though she had actually done so, Daniel turned and smiled at her. 'Happy?'

'Yes, I am.'

'Isn't it a wonderful feeling? I never knew it till I joined the Revelationists.'

'They mean a great deal to you, don't they?'

'Everything,' he said simply.

'If you had to state your beliefs, Daniel, exactly what would they be?'

'I believe in a new heaven and a new earth. That's our

basic creed. In the early days of the Movement we were known as the Neo Celestians.'

'But a new heaven and earth where?'

'Here—heaven on earth, a new world, where God and man live together.'

'And woman!' Nina said with a smile.

'As it says in legal documents, "*Man* shall embrace *woman*"! I'm so thankful you found us, Nina,' he went on more seriously. 'We need people like you—I knew it at once, and Brad confirmed it.'

'Brad?'

'He's a psychologist, didn't you know? He screens potential recruits for us and advises us to reject those he thinks unsuitable.'

'But I thought you wanted everyone you could get?'

'Up to a point that's true, but sometimes we get people who are unstable, or who aren't genuine and want to make trouble. With Brad's help, we can root them out before they infiltrate. And he also picks out those he thinks capable of becoming leaders. The vast majority never will, but that's not important. They've been saved, and they bring in others. Noah's ravens and doves, we call them.

'You, though, have an air of authority; people would follow you unquestioningly. Brad thinks you could rise as high as Pastor or even Prelate.'

Privately—and with some relief—Nina doubted Brad's judgement. He'd not spotted her as an infiltrator, which she'd undoubtedly been in the beginning. Or had he seen beneath initial suspicion to a deeper commitment? The thought made her uncomfortable; though she admired the Movement, she was not ready to commit herself. She therefore threw a pebble into his certainty.

'I thought God promised there wouldn't be another Flood?'

Daniel remained untroubled. 'That's an inaccuracy in translation. And as I explained, it won't be total devastation this time. Thousands of us around the world will survive, with the majority of animals.'

Nina remembered Webb's suggestion of water-wings. 'How? The animals, I mean?'

'It's not for us to question, Nina, simply to accept.'

'And what about the millions of people who'll perish?'

He shrugged. 'We're giving as many as possible the chance to join us, but the Devil's had it his own way for too long; the majority have drifted into his camp.'

Nina paused to look behind her at the sun-bathed landscape. It seemed odd in such a setting to be talking about the Devil and all his works.

'You must meet a fair bit of hostility,' she said. 'Does it bother you?'

'In a way it makes things easier, by showing up the Devil's agents.'

Nina said incredulously, 'You believe that everyone who opposes you works for the Devil?'

He looked surprised. 'Of course. I should have thought that was obvious.'

She opened her mouth to protest, but perhaps fortunately Alice's voice reached them as she came running back to ask if it was lunch-time, and the moment passed.

Having collected the picnic hamper from the car, they found a hollow out of the wind and settled down to enjoy their lunch. But Nina, only half-listening to her daughter's chatter, was still considering Daniel's statements of belief. When expounded by Noah Bellringer they had seemed acceptable, even convincing; now, on this sunlit afternoon, they appeared suddenly full of threat.

When the meal was over, Alice took her skipping rope to the far side of the hollow and embarked on a complicated routine.

'It could be a scene out of the past, couldn't it?' Daniel commented, leaning on his elbow as he watched her. 'A little girl called Alice and her skipping rope—part of an older, safer world.'

'What was the little boys' equivalent? Marbles?'

He shrugged. 'I'm not much of an authority on childhood, since I never really had one.'

Nina lay back on the warm grass. 'How so?'

'I was illegitimate, and the fact that I came from "a good family" made it worse. After a year or two my mother married an American and went to live in the States.'

'Leaving you behind?'

He nodded, his eyes still on Alice's flying legs.

'But what happened to you?'

'My grandmother brought me up. She was kind enough, but I always felt I was a nuisance. When I was eight I was sent to boarding school, where the other boys teased me because I didn't live with my parents like everyone else. It wasn't a particularly happy childhood.'

'You never felt part of a family?'

'Not till I joined the Movement. That was the turning point, for the others as well as me. We're all damaged in some way, but being together gives us a sense of worth, of belonging. Nothing and no one, Nina, is more important than the Captain and his vision of a better world. Never forget that.'

Nina, who'd been watching his face during this speech, saw the feverish gleam in his eyes and was disturbed by it. Faith, she thought, was one thing, fanaticism another. And as though to underline her unease a cloud suddenly raced across the sun, plunging their hollow into shadow and switching the warmth to a sudden coolness which presaged autumn.

She shivered. There wouldn't be many more picnics this year. By mutual consent they gathered their things together and set off back to the car.

On the drive home, Nina remembered that wild moment of happiness up on the ridge, but it was as though it had happened to someone else.

'Hannah! Bless you for coming.'

Dilys seized her arm and drew her into the house. 'She's out with the baby at the moment but they're always back by four-thirty. He has half an hour's "playtime" before his bath, after which he's fed and put down at six. I can set my watch by it.'

'I thought such rigorous time-keeping was out of fashion.'

'Fashion or not, he's the most contented baby I've ever come across.'

'Which,' Hannah teased, 'isn't saying much. Does he sleep through the night?'

'So Susie maintains. Certainly I've never heard him.'

Hannah settled herself on the sofa. 'Well, tell me about the girl. What's worrying you?'

'For one thing she's so self-contained and secretive—like an automaton, almost. Totally unapproachable.'

'And that's a problem? I thought your main concern was that she'd get in your way?'

'Don't rub it in, Hannah, I know I'm being illogical. But I did at least expect a friendly smile if we met on the stairs.'

'Which you don't get?'

'No, just a cool nod as she hurries past.' Dilys paused. 'Mind you, I probably got her back up the other day, when I went to her room.'

'Why did you do that?'

'To see what she was doing,' Dilys said bluntly. 'Though I made the excuse of offering her coffee.'

'And what *was* she doing? Stirring toads' eyes into a cauldron?'

Dilys smiled sheepishly. 'Working, as Susie said. The dressing-table was being used as a desk and there were papers and text books everywhere. She said she was writing a treatise.'

'And she suspected you of spying on her?'

'Quite probably.'

Hannah shook her head. 'I still don't get it. She keeps out of your way—no doubt obeying Susie's stringent instructions—the baby doesn't disturb you, and you say she's marvellous with him. Why can't you just relax and get on with your book?'

'You think I'm making excuses, don't you?'

'Aren't you?' Hannah challenged her.

'Not really, though I confess the block's still there. But dammit, when I agreed she could come to the house, I did at least expect a human being!'

There was a tap on the door and Peggy came in with the tea-tray. As she left the room, Hannah nodded after her.

'Any friction there?'

'None whatever, but Peggy's enslaved by the baby. I even overheard her begging to be allowed to bath him.'

'Well, I honestly can't see what's worrying you.'

Dilys poured tea from the silver pot. 'Wait till you see her, then you can decide for yourself. And if you think I'm going round the twist and she's a perfectly normal young woman, then I'll abide by what you say and swallow my misgivings. In the meantime, let's talk of something else. What about that member of staff you were worried about?'

'Don't ask!' Hannah said darkly, taking her cup and saucer. 'I braced myself to have a talk with her, and she has looked marginally neater since. Then, yesterday, she collapsed in class.'

'Good grief! What caused that?'

'Nervous exhaustion, according to John Templeton, accentuated by malnutrition. I told you she hardly ate a thing.'

'But what's the matter with her?'

'Lord knows. A complete breakdown, I shouldn't wonder.'

'Mental, you mean?'

'And physical. *Why* did this have to happen while Gwen's away?'

'Where is she now?'

'In the san.'

'So what happens next?'

'I wish I knew. We'll wait and see what John advises.'

'Perhaps,' Dilys said rallyingly, 'it's nothing serious, and a weekend in bed will put her right.'

'Let us devoutly hope so.'

The sound of the front door reached them, and Dilys tensed. 'There they are now.'

She stood up quickly, rocking the small tea-table as she hurried to the door. Hannah heard her say with false brightness, 'Miss Baines, would you bring the baby into the sitting-room? I have a friend here, and she'd very much like to see him.'

Hannah caught only a murmured reply but when, a moment later, the young woman followed Dilys unsmilingly into the room, the baby in her arms, she felt a jolt of surprise. It was the woman she'd seen talking to Miss Hendrix outside the library.

As Dilys introduced the nanny, she wondered whether to mention this, but decided against it. Instead, she said pleasantly, 'I'm delighted to meet this young man. His mother was one of my star pupils at Ashbourne.'

Sarah Baines smiled fleetingly, coming forward so Hannah could see the baby more clearly. He regarded her with the disconcerting gaze of the very young, and Hannah, while talking to him and stroking his smooth round cheek and dimpled fist, unobtrusively took stock of his nanny.

As Dilys had said, there was a standoffish air about her which might possibly mask shyness. She was tall and pale, her hair severely pulled back, her dress plain and without ornament. Like a Quaker, Hannah thought. But the look of almost yearning tenderness with which she regarded her charge was strangely moving. Dilys was right there; whatever else this strange young woman might do or not do, she would never harm the child.

Sebastian, who had stoically withstood Hannah's attentions, became bored with them and turned his head away. Sarah said quietly, 'I'll take him upstairs now,' and with a nod at the two women, carried him out of the room.

'Not "if you don't mind" or "if that's all right", you notice,' Dilys commented, returning to her cooling cup of tea. 'Just "I'll take him upstairs." Well—' she looked steadily at Hannah—'what's the verdict?'

Hannah said, 'She's different, I'll grant you that.'

Dilys was watching her closely. 'And?'

'A rather strange coincidence. I saw her in town a week

ago talking to Miss Hendrix, the member of staff who's collapsed.'

Dilys gave a bark of laughter. 'So your problem and my problem are connected. How tidy!'

But Hannah wasn't smiling. Because Miss Hendrix, too, seemed set apart from the rest of them, the very quality that had disturbed Dilys in the nanny. And now it appeared they knew each other. Had their strangeness evolved from the same source?

Dilys said quietly, 'I wasn't imagining it, was I?'

'No, I don't think you were, but there's nothing you can do. If Susie's satisfied with her and she's good with the baby—'

'She raises the hairs on the back of my neck.'

'Ignore it—you have to. Go back to your book and shut everything else out of your mind. If you don't think about her she'll go away—in two weeks, if not before. And now,' Hannah said firmly, as Dilys started to protest, 'perhaps I could have another cup of tea?'

CHAPTER 11

WDS Sally Pierce looked helplessly at the weeping woman across the desk. Probably the claustrophobic atmosphere of the interview room was intimidating, but there was nowhere else to take her. The two little girls, aged roughly four and six, hung on to their mother's coat and surveyed Sally with wide, frightened eyes.

'Mrs Palmer,' she said gently, 'please try to stop crying. It's upsetting the children.'

'But I don't know what to *do!*' the woman sobbed. She raised her head and made an ineffectual attempt to dry her eyes. 'I'm sorry, but I've kept going for months now, hoping it would all come right. Today I've had to face the fact that it won't.'

'Try to tell me what happened,' Sally prompted.

Mrs Palmer was continuing with her own line of thought. 'What I can't understand is Trevor being taken in by these people—believing in them, I mean. He's an intelligent man, he has a degree and is—was—a partner in his computer firm. But these last months he's changed unbelievably. He gave up his job and spends all his time going round trying to convert people before it's "too late". And worst of all, he seems to think I'm *evil*.'

She started weeping again. This time Sally let her continue until she herself made an effort at control.

'They seemed so nice at first,' she said then, 'friendly and kind. But when they realized I didn't want to join them, they changed completely. They told Trevor I'd been sent by Satan to deflect him from the true path to God. *Satan!*' she repeated hysterically. 'I didn't think people talked like that any more. And now Trevor's withdrawn all our savings, and made it over to them, and there doesn't seem to be anything I can do about it! All he can talk about is this Noah Bellringer, who's coming over here. I wish I could get my hands on him!'

Sally repeated the conversation to Webb later. 'I gave her that address that's on the board, Guv. Do you think they'll be able to help her?'

'More than we can, at any rate.'

'But surely she's exaggerating? It seems amazing that in this day and age—'

'This day and age is the whole trouble, Sally,' Webb said heavily. 'People feel let down by accepted religions and they're desperate enough to believe anything.'

'But he's an educated man, Mr Palmer, he's not—'

'They're the ones most at risk. These cults are very convincing, you know; they appeal to people with a social conscience, who are "caring", in the modern jargon. But if anything conflicts with their *raison d'être*—which is what their religion is—they can be as ruthless and single-minded as any other fanatics. Because that's what they are, Sally, make no mistake. They're fanatics, and very dangerous.'

Sally said helplessly, 'But can't we *do* anything?'

'Not unless they break the law. Mrs Palmer's right there; if her husband wants to give up everything and join the Revvies, there's nothing either she or we can do to stop him.'

There had been a heavy dew overnight and the grass was still drenched. Hannah walked slowly down the school drive, delighting in the shimmering spiders' webs, studded with drops of water, which festooned every bush. Berries clustered thickly, and overhead the leaves were turning colour, deepening from yellow through rust to deepest red.

Normally, she loved this time of year but at the moment problems were pressing too heavily on her for any real enjoyment. As she was leaving her study just now, Charles had phoned to finalize the arrangements for Friday. She was still not sure she'd done right in accepting, and hoped he wouldn't take it as encouragement. Also, the Frenches were sure to be there, and that could be embarrassing.

Which brought her back to her problems. She was not naïve enough to imagine that, with their cassettes and pamphlets confiscated, the girls would forget their experiences and revert to normal. Phone-calls and mail were monitored, but she had the uneasy feeling that such measures would prove no match for the Revvies. Somehow, they would contrive to keep up their pressure on potential recruits until they had their full allegiance.

She had reached the gate and stood for a moment, drawing in the still, clear air. Ashbourne School stood in prime position in the curve of the crescent that was Montpellier Gardens and immediately opposite its gates were the small, railed gardens to which all the residents held a key. Occasionally, when she was free and the school grounds were noisy with tennis or hockey matches, Hannah came here to read through her papers or a book, sometimes merely to sit under the trees and recharge her batteries, grateful for its green quietness. Now, however, she was on a specific errand, and turned to her right to follow the crescent round to the school boarding houses.

Austen and Brontë Houses were adjacent to each other in their own grounds, each accommodating fifty boarders, and a single-storey annexe to Austen formed the school sanatorium. It was there that Hannah was bound.

The school employed three trained nurses who were known by the title of 'Matron', one based in the school building and one in each of the boarding houses. Unless there was an epidemic, when extra nursing staff were called in, they shared the care of sanatorium patients between them.

Hannah turned into Austen's gateway and walked down the drive alongside the house to the annexe at the end of it—a drive wide enough, should need arise, to allow an ambulance access. They had had their share of faulty tonsils and appendixes over the years but thankfully seldom anything more serious.

Janet Rimmer, Brontë's matron, was on duty at the desk in the wide entrance hall, and she rose as Hannah entered. 'Good morning, Miss James.'

'Good morning. I've called to see how Miss Hendrix is.'

Miss Rimmer shook her head doubtfully. 'The doctor's due later today, but I'm concerned about her. She's desperate to go home.'

'Is she eating?'

'A little.'

Hannah indicated the basket she held. 'I've brought fruit rather than flowers, in the hope of tempting her. Which room is she in?'

'Four, just down the passage. Shall I—?'

'No, don't trouble, I'll find my own way.'

She walked down the corridor, tapped lightly on the door and, receiving no response, pushed it open. The room was small and bright, with sunshine pouring through the window. Mattie Hendrix lay like a small bird on the high hospital bed, her face as white as the pillow beneath it. On seeing Hannah, she hastily struggled into a sitting position, clutching the sheet against her bony breast.

'Oh, Miss James—how kind.'

'Please—there's no need to sit up. I've brought you some fruit.' She set it down on the cabinet alongside the bed and Mattie murmured confused thanks. 'Are you feeling a little better?'

'I'm fine—just fine. I feel a complete fraud lying here causing so much bother.' Her thin face flushed. 'I'm so very sorry about Friday—I can't think what came over me. What must the class have thought?'

'They were concerned, as you see.' Hannah had caught sight of the large 'Get Well' card propped on the windowsill.

'After all these years of teaching, to lose control like that—it's unbelievable. I assure you it won't happen again.'

'I'm sure it won't, but in the meantime you need looking after until you're back to yourself again.'

'But I am—I've fully recovered. In fact, I asked Matron if she'd have some books sent in for me to be working on, but she refused.'

'I should think so,' Hannah said, smiling to dissipate the sternness of her words. 'You're here to rest and build up your strength.' Privately, she could appreciate Matron's concern; there was a feverishness about the patient, a kind of urgency, which was disquieting and indicated that the reason for her collapse might be more deep-seated than they'd realized.

'But you'll impress on Dr Templeton that I'm quite well?' she was insisting. 'I so dislike being behind with my work, both for the school and my personal affairs.'

'I'll have a word with him, but of course the decision is his.' And yet, thought Hannah, if the woman was fretting so much to get back, she was unlikely to improve under enforced confinement.

She stayed a few minutes more, chatting generally about

school affairs, and as she left, had to promise again to put in a word with the doctor.

Janet Rimmer rose anxiously as Hannah approached the entrance hall. 'What did you think?'

'I agree with you—I don't like the look of her. Would you ask Dr Templeton to come to the school when he's seen her?'

'Of course.' The Matron hesitated. 'Forgive my asking, Miss James, but did you take that business of the cassette any further?'

'Yes, I spoke to the girls, without any notable success, and had their parents in to see me.'

'Were they concerned?'

'Yes, I think we can say they're concerned. There haven't been any further incidents?'

'No. The girls are always in corners whispering together, but then they always have been.'

'But none of the others seem to be involved?'

'Not that I've noticed.'

'We'll just have to hope we've nipped it in the bud,' said Hannah, and trusted she sounded more positive than she felt.

When Sally had left him, Webb sat staring gloomily at the pile of papers in front of him. Statements had now been collected from virtually everyone who'd been at the King's Head last Monday, but no further light shed on the mysterious couple with whom Kershaw had left the bar.

The rest of the feelers he'd put out were meeting with varying degrees of success. A taxi-driver based at the station remembered taking a fare to Calder's Close around ten-thirty last Monday, which confirmed what they'd already guessed. Kershaw's wife was being asked for the name of his solicitors; it would have been natural for him to contact them after seeing Soames.

The other French inquiries had proved negative: Kershaw had been happily married and respected in his neighbourhood. Though known in local gambling circles, he'd always met his debts and was regarded as a good sportsman.

As he reached for another pile of papers, a separate report caught Webb's eye and he pulled it towards him. It was the lab's analysis of Hannah's cassette and he read through it with interest. It seemed there was indeed subliminal information on the tape, the words *love, trust, salvation* being inserted at regular intervals, together with sounds of rushing water. More disturbingly, disjointed words such as *Satan, danger* and *punishment* also occurred, guaranteed to cause anxiety and the desire to conform. On the face of it, there seemed no reason not to incorporate them openly on the soundtrack, but Webb conceded grimly that there was method in it: messages received subliminally had more impact, became accepted as instincts and memories of one's own.

Still, he'd need more than that before he could touch the Revvies, so there was no point in wasting any more time on them. Nor was he getting anywhere sitting around here. He needed to be out in the thick of the investigation, wherever that might be.

'Ken?'

'Yes, Guv?' Jackson appeared at the door.

'We're going walkabout, in search of inspiration.'

Jackson grinned. 'If you say so, Guv.'

Webb worked out his plan as they went down the stairs. 'We'll go back to the solicitor's office and retrace the route Kershaw would have taken on his way to the King's Head. Since he doesn't appear to have made any phone-calls, perhaps he dropped in somewhere or bumped into someone *en route*. Let's hope something will obligingly leap up and hit us in the eye.'

The October sun shone warmly, a true Indian summer. Women were still in cotton dresses and an ice-cream van, glad of the prolonged season, sounded its carillon as it passed them.

They walked briskly along Carrington Street and turned into Franklyn Road, one of Shillingham's business centres.

It also contained two pubs well known to the men of Carrington Street, the Brown Bear, favoured by CID, at the lower end, and the Red Lion halfway down. Jackson hoped their proximity would not escape the Governor, since the lunch hour was fast approaching.

Webb came to a halt outside the offices of Culpepper, Soames & Soames. 'Right. No need to go in. Now, Kershaw came out here and, making for the King's Head, would obviously turn to his right.' The two men started walking again. 'And here,' Webb said, 'we come to our first problem.'

He paused on the corner of a small road running from Franklyn Road to parallel Duke Street. 'Now, Ken. If you were going to the King's Head, would you turn down here or go on to the end and along King Street?'

Jackson shrugged. 'It's as broad as it's long, Guv.'

'Then we'll do both,' said Webb inexorably.

'Mind you,' Jackson added, seeing his pie and pint fade into the distance, 'if he was a stranger round here—and he was, these days—I should think he'd carry straight on—it's the more direct route.'

'Right, then we'll try that first. Now, keep your eyes peeled for anything that might have distracted him.'

'Ten to one it was someone he met by chance in the street.'

'Not many chance encounters lead to that kind of murder. A quick stab in the ribs or a knock over the head, maybe, but not an injection with a ready-prepared syringe.'

They crossed the narrow road and, to Jackson's regret, passed the Red Lion on the corner. 'Now, look about you, Ken. See anything promising?'

Jackson obediently halted and looked. 'Well, there's the Art Centre across the way there. He could have gone into the picture gallery or the library.'

'Wouldn't have had time, not if he left Soames at twelve-fifteen and was in the bar about twelve-forty, having already been to his room.'

'So he couldn't have popped into the Town Hall or the

swimming baths either,' Jackson commented, as those buildings came into sight.

'Hardly.'

In a depressed silence they walked on until they reached busy King Street and turned in the direction of Gloucester Circus.

'You can see the hotel on the far corner down there, so let's suppose he crossed over straight away.'

They waited for the traffic lights to change and made their way across the road. But as they reached the pavement Jackson stopped suddenly, causing Webb to cannon into him.

'Look out, Ken! What are you playing at?'

'If he *did* cross here, Guv, look what was staring him in the face.'

Webb turned and saw one of the new glass telephone booths against the wall.

'Perhaps,' Jackson went on, his voice ringing with excitement, '*that's* how he fixed the meeting. On the spur of the moment, like.'

'You could be right,' Webb said slowly. 'Well spotted, Ken. So we're back to a phone-call rather than a chance meeting—which was always the more likely bet. But also back to the sixty-four thousand dollar question—who did he arrange to meet?'

'We could talk through the possibilities over lunch,' Jackson suggested hopefully.

Webb grinned. 'OK, point taken. But who *could* he have phoned, Ken? He didn't know anyone but Soames, and he'd just left him.'

They began walking again. 'Let's get back to his state of mind. He's just heard that the legacy he'd been staking everything on wasn't going to him after all but to an obscure cult he'd probably never heard of. Suddenly he sees a phone box. Who does he ring?'

'His solicitors?'

'Quite probably; but he couldn't have fixed a meeting straight away, because they're in London. Any other ideas?'

'The Revvies,' Jackson said promptly. 'To try to talk them round.'

Webb's eyes narrowed. 'He wouldn't have their number.'

'His mother might have, and he'd just been to her house, remember. He could have taken her address book or phone pad. Or he might have found one of those publicity sheets like DI Petrie gave you. Come to that, they could even be in the book.'

Webb clapped him round the shoulder. 'Ken, you're a wonder. That could well be the answer. There's nothing I'd like better than to involve the Revvies in this business— it'd give us a legit chance to go for them. But proving it will be tricky. Whoever it was, they've covered their tracks too well. And in all conscience I can't think why they'd want to kill Kershaw. They had the money, after all; he was more likely to try to kill them. Still, it's given us a different angle, and you've more than earned your pint.'

'Sister Matilda!'

The commanding voice rang out as Mattie was hurrying to the front door with replacement cassettes for the girls. She considered making a dash for it, but her legs wouldn't have carried her. Fearfully, she turned to face Brad Lübekker.

'Yes, Prelate?'

'I understand your last three instalments are still outstanding?'

'Well, yes, but it was only Thursday you spoke to me. I was taken ill on Friday and spent the weekend in the sanatorium. In fact, I should still be there, but I refused to stay.' She looked anxiously into his cold, implacable eyes.

'If you remember, Thursday was your final warning. When so many are waiting for your place, we can't have you reneging on your payments.'

Tears flooded her eyes and the dreaded trembling started again, as it had in the classroom on Friday. 'I'm not reneging! I'll get it somehow, I promise—'

'It's too late for promises. As you know, the Captain

arrives in England this evening and we've heard we're to be honoured with a personal visit on Saturday. Naturally, we want everything to be in order, so I'll give you another twenty-four hours. If you fail to make the payment in that time, you'll have to justify yourself to the Captain.'

She gazed at him aghast. 'No! I'll do anything—'

'It's in your own hands, Sister. Now, you must excuse me. I have work to do.'

Dilys had spent the afternoon at the library, doing a spot of much-needed research. After Hannah's visit on Saturday she had determined to take her advice and put all doubts about Sarah Baines out of her head. It was getting her nowhere and seriously interfering with her work. And as Hannah had said, as long as Sebastian was safe with the girl, nothing else mattered. Consequently when Susie had phoned from Japan the previous evening she'd been able to report, with fewer reservations than before, that all was well.

Having taken herself in hand, she had just passed a profitable few hours which would stand her in good stead and might well break the block which had been plaguing her these past weeks. All in all, she felt happier and more settled than at any time since she'd learned of the proposed invasion.

The rush-hour traffic was in full swing and she glanced at her watch. A quarter to six—later than she realized. Back at the house the baby would be almost ready to put down. And what, she wondered, would the enigmatic Miss Baines be doing this evening—working on her 'treatise' or visiting her cousin in the town? They must be a pretty close family to spend so much time together.

Dilys reached Lethbridge Road with a sigh of relief, thinking pleasurably of the large gin and tonic she would pour herself as a reward for returning to work. Then, as she rounded the bend just before Hassocks, she saw a man standing at her gate. It was no one she recognized.

She indicated right, and, seeing she intended to drive in,

he hurried to open the gates for her and stood to one side
to let her pass. Dilys wound down her window.

'Good evening,' she said, 'can I help you?'

He bent down towards her—an attractive-looking man
in his forties with the kind of craggy, lived-in face which
had always appealed to her.

'You must be Miss Hayward. Good evening, ma'am.'
His accent surprised her; there were not many Americans
in Shillingham. 'Thank you kindly but no, I shan't trouble
you. I'm waiting for Sarah—I guess she'll be out any
minute.'

'You're her cousin?' Dilys was aware of disappointment.

He smiled. 'That's right, ma'am, Brad Lübekker. Glad
to know you.'

'How do you do?' Dilys said uncertainly, added, 'I don't
suppose she'll be long', and with a vague smile drove on
towards the garage. When she got out to open the doors,
he had moved discreetly back behind the gate post. Should
she have invited him in, she wondered as she emerged from
the garage. But before she could decide, Sarah Baines came
hurrying out of the house, stopping in surprise as she caught
sight of Dilys.

'Oh, Miss Hayward. I've just put Sebastian down, so I
hope—'

Dilys said steadily, 'Your cousin's waiting at the gate.'

'Oh! Thank you.' And she hurried down the path, leaving
Dilys staring after her. Because something in her face had,
to Dilys's observant eye, made one fact abundantly clear.

'Cousin be damned!' she said out loud. 'They're *lovers*,
for God's sake! That man is her lover!'

For some reason her fingers were shaking slightly as she
put her key in the door and pushed it open. She dropped
her sheaf of notes on to the hall table, trying to adjust to
a changed image of Sarah Baines. That cold, unsmiling,
unadorned young woman had a lover—and an attractive
one, at that. She must, Dilys reflected grimly, have hidden
depths.

She walked into the sitting-room and poured herself a

generous gin and tonic, adding a slice of lemon and ice from the silver bucket Peggy had left ready. Then, with the tall glass chilling her fingers, she went to the telephone.

'Hannah? You'll never guess what! Nanny Baines has an admirer!'

Over the wire she heard Hannah's light laugh. 'You phoned to tell me that?'

'Well, it staggered me more than somewhat. She looks as though she hasn't an ounce of emotion in her.'

'Except with the baby,' Hannah reminded her.

'Except with the baby,' Dilys agreed.

'Well, go on. How do you know? Have you seen him?'

Dilys recounted the brief meeting at the gate, ending, 'What surprised me most is how attractive he is. American, too—I wonder where she met him. Anyway, it explains the number of evenings she goes into town to meet her "cousin". I wonder if Susie knows?'

After she'd replaced the receiver, she stood looking down at it for a moment. Still waters run deep, she thought, and then, for no reason she could pinpoint, shivered suddenly.

On an impulse she put down her glass and went upstairs to the baby's bedroom. The curtains were drawn but there was sufficient light from the landing for her to make her way over to the cot. Sebastian was not yet asleep. He lay contentedly on his back, one fist waving in the air as he cooed softly to himself. A faint smell of warm milk and talcum powder reached her nostrils.

Unable to distinguish her face in the half-light, he stared up at her, as if waiting for her to make a move.

She said softly, 'I haven't made you very welcome, have I, but I hope you're enjoying your visit.' Bending down, she retrieved a small furry toy which had become wedged in the bars of the cot and laid it by the baby's side.

'Good night, Sebastian. Sleep well.'

He lay looking unblinkingly up at her. Then he gave a little gurgle and, totally unexpectedly, treated her to a toothless smile. She touched his cheek with one finger, reminding herself of the conditions under which she tolerated babies.

'Good night, poppet,' she said, and quietly left the room.

It was seven o'clock when Webb pressed the doorbell at No. 5, Victoria Drive. By now, he considered, they should all have returned to the coop, and it was all of them that he intended to see.

As before, Reed opened the door to them, raising his eyebrows as he took in not only Webb and Jackson but Dawson, Cummings and Marshbanks behind them. 'Reinforcements, Chief Inspector?'

'Simply to speed things up, sir. We have a bit of checking to do, and would be most grateful for your cooperation.'

'You'd better come in, then.'

This time—possibly because there were more of them—they were taken into the larger room on the left, which was furnished with groups of wooden chairs and tables. It did not, Jackson thought, look particularly inviting.

'I believe you said there were eight of you in the house, sir?'

'That's right.'

'Is everyone here at the moment?'

'Yes, I was the last in—you've just caught me.' He smiled. 'In a manner of speaking. Actually they're in the kitchen; we were just about to start supper.'

'Excellent. Then DC Marshbanks can supervise proceedings from there.' He turned to Marshbanks. 'Send one person along in the first instance, Constable, and we'll start with Mr Reed here. The rest of them can carry on with their supper. When the first two get back, send the next lot. We'll have them in two by two,' he added, deadpan, 'like the animals going into the Ark.'

There was no flicker of response from Reed.

'Now, Sergeant Dawson,' Webb continued, 'if you and DC Cummings conduct your interviews over by those folding doors, we won't disturb each other.'

Marshbanks turned to Adam. 'Could you tell me where the kitchen is, sir?'

'At the end of the passage,' he said tightly, then, to Webb, 'I told you all I know the other day.'

'Different questions, sir,' Webb said implacably. 'If you'd like to sit down, we won't keep you from your supper longer than necessary.'

The aim of the questioning this time was to ascertain where they'd all been at lunch-time last Monday. By immediately cutting off the chance to confer, Webb hoped to have pre-empted any fabrication of alibis.

But it appeared, as the interviews progressed, that most of them had jobs outside the group, which occupied them during the day. Reed managed a shoe shop in the town centre, Daniel Stacey taught PE at the Grammar School, while Terry Doble and Vince Merrick, who had made themselves so invaluable to Mrs Kershaw, worked at a youth centre.

One after another they produced genuine-sounding alibis which, though they would be checked, sounded depressingly watertight.

Two of the four girls also had jobs, as dental nurse and receptionist respectively, but two—Lucy, whom they'd already met, and Liz Fenchurch, were unemployed. They were the only two out of the eight who admitted to being in the house at lunch-time on Monday, and they denied all knowledge of a phone-call. Looking at them, Webb had in any case the greatest difficulty in imagining them injecting poison into anyone.

But that was the damnable thing, he thought in frustration. They all seemed polite, friendly young people. It began to look as though Ken's bright idea would not hold water after all.

'Are there any other members of your sect?' Webb asked Reed when, after the others had been dismissed, he returned at Webb's request.

The man smiled. 'Most certainly, Chief Inspector. Dozens are joining us every day. If you want to interview

all of them, it might be simpler to go through the Electoral
Register.'

Webb rose wearily to his feet, signalling to the others
down the room. 'Very well, Mr Reed, that will be all for
the moment. We'll be in touch if we need anything further.'

CHAPTER 12

Webb was still turning over the interviews in his head when
he arrived back at the flat. It was after nine—rather late
to invite Hannah to dinner, but worth a try. He dialled her
number, but it was the answerphone that replied and he
left a brief message and hung up, aware of disappointment.
He felt like cooking something special, and it would have
been pleasant to share it. None the less, he decided to go
ahead.

After pouring himself a drink, he opened the fridge and
surveyed the two chicken breasts which awaited him, dis-
carding the plebian options of frying or grilling and mentally running through half a dozen other possibilities.

When he and his wife divorced eight years ago he had
painstakingly taught himself to cook, chiefly by adapting
recipes in the *Broadshire Evening News*. It was a form of
relaxation and one he enjoyed. Hannah maintained that
the more complicated a case became, the more elaborate
his cuisine.

Spiced, he decided now, rather than Maryland or Kiev.
They'd need to marinate for half an hour, but he wanted
another look at those alibis and he might as well get them
out of the way before the meal.

Reaching for garlic and fresh ginger, he methodically set
to work, the small glass of whisky at his side. Had he mis-
judged the Revvies? Could they really be the dangerous
fanatics about whom he'd warned Nina and Sally? Or was
he himself fanatical in so distrusting them?

Leaving the chicken to marinate, he carried his whisky

into the living-room, sat down in his favourite chair and began to go through his notes. He'd detailed Bob Dawson to arrange for the checking of alibis, but at first glance the only one with the opportunity of calling at the King's Head at lunch-time was Daniel Stacey, who admitted to having been 'canvassing', albeit at the other end of town.

Webb took another sip of whisky. What, he wondered, had led that oddly assorted but pleasant-seeming bunch of people to join the sect? What particular aspect had appealed to each of them?

For the younger girls, it could have been the warm, family feeling or the security of a strong leader; for the men, a worthwhile job to do; for them all, perhaps, the certainty of salvation.

They'd all admitted knowing of Kershaw's existence, but only after reading of his death in the paper. Could he believe that? It was hard to think any of them were lying. Perhaps after all it had been Kershaw's misfortune to fall in with two homicidal maniacs who had no connection with the Revvies or anyone else. In which case they had damn-all chance of finding them.

Christina sat staring unseeingly at the television screen in which her husband seemed so engrossed. Ever since their meeting with Miss James she'd felt unsettled, almost as though waiting for some disaster to befall them. In fact, she'd written a long letter to Stephie—a rare occurrence indeed—begging her to have nothing more to do with the cult and setting out in detail the dangers inherent in it. Of course, there had been no reply.

So what could they do, she wondered. In view of the seriousness of the matter, would they be allowed to go and see her? Even have her home again for the weekend? Though that could be unwise; she might slip out of their grasp and return to the Revelationists, possibly for good this time. And suppose it was all still hanging fire when term broke up? Neither she nor Edward could act as chaperone for the three long weeks of the Christmas holidays.

She stirred restlessly. She'd read stories in the press about distraught relatives whose children had been sucked into a cult, only to turn against them and refuse to come home. And in all conscience, theirs had not been a close family to start with. Herself and Edward, yes, but not the children. Looking back, the children had always been on the outside. *Mea culpa*, she thought miserably.

Think of something else! But as she closed her mind to that problem, another manifested itself, and against the flickering screen she saw again the attractive, smiling face of the man who'd offered to buy her a drink and then, unbelievably, got himself murdered. It seemed the police had still not found his killers.

Suppose, she thought suddenly, they had been in the bar earlier than everyone thought, and had seen her talking to Philip Kershaw? They might be wondering if he'd told her anything—who he was expecting, for instance? Might the killers now be looking for her, with the aim of silencing her?

'Edward, I'm frightened,' she said.

'Um?' His eyes were still on the television.

'I said, I'm frightened!' she repeated, raising her voice. He turned towards her, struggling to detach his mind from the serial he'd been following.

'Frightened? Darling, whatever of?'

'Of what's going to happen to Stephie, and to me if the killers saw me speaking to that man.'

Edward pressed the remote control and the screen went blank. He got up and came to sit beside her, putting an arm round her shoulder. 'Sweetheart, I'd no idea you'd been brooding like that. Why didn't you say?'

'Aren't *you* worried?' she challenged him.

'I'm concerned about Stephie, yes, but it never struck me you were in danger. In fact, I'm quite sure you're not. If the killers did see you, which I doubt, they'd realize you've had plenty of time to pass on any information, so there's no point in coming after you now.'

She relaxed against him. 'I suppose not. But what can

we do about those people Stephie's involved with? We can't watch her all through the Christmas holidays.'

'If they're still around, we'll go away for Christmas,' Edward said firmly.

'For three weeks? Will you be able to spare the time?'

'Most certainly, if that's what it takes to keep her out of their clutches. What about you?'

There were a dozen reasons why she didn't want to be away over Christmas, but she bit them back. Perhaps it was time she put her daughter before her own inclinations—Miss James evidently thought so.

'The same, of course,' she answered. Then she reached up to kiss his mouth. 'What would I do without you?' she said.

The subject of the Revvies was also under discussion at the Chases' home, though less amicably.

'It's obvious your precious Miss James hasn't a very high opinion of us,' Diane was saying.

Gordon stirred defensively. 'What do you mean, *my* Miss James?'

'Oh come on, I know you fancy her. All those smouldering looks you throw in her direction—it's pathetic.'

He flushed angrily. 'You're becoming neurotic, you know that?'

'And who made me like that? You and your lady-friends, that's who!'

'For God's sake!'

'Look, I didn't mean to start a slanging match, I just want us to talk about Marina. Suppose she's really involved with that cult.'

Gordon fished in his pocket and withdrew the card Hannah had given him. 'We could always contact these people and see what they say.'

'I feel so guilty,' Diane said miserably. 'We've been so wrapped up in our own problems we've neglected the children. And now this happens.'

'They're hardly ever here anyway.'

'That's partly the trouble. I know your parents meant well, but I *wish* they hadn't taken out those policies. We'd all have been much closer if the children had been at Grammar School and home every evening.'

'It was while Marina was home that all this happened,' Gordon pointed out.

'And Miss James blames us—she made it plain enough. I always get a complex when I go to that hateful school.' Diane was close to tears. 'And this time it was worse than ever. I could see her comparing me with Christina French, all tarted up in her designer clothes.'

'What rubbish!' Gordon said explosively. 'Miss James has better things to do than worry about whether you're wearing last year's model. Anyway, Christina didn't come out of it any better than we did. Rather worse, in fact.'

His voice softened. 'I know you never wanted private schools, but Mum and Dad scrimped and saved for years to make it possible. They couldn't manage it for me, but they were determined to for the kids.'

'I know, but they should have *asked* us, instead of just announcing it. If they'd wanted to help out, I'd rather have used the money for music lessons, or riding, or something like that—extras we couldn't have provided ourselves at that stage.'

'Don't be so bloody ungrateful! Most people would give their eye teeth to get their kids into Ashbourne and Greystones.'

Diane's hands clenched in her lap. 'You haven't answered my question,' she said tightly. 'What are we going to *do*?'

'Hope it'll blow over, I suppose. Girls that age are always getting crazes. Ten to one she'll be into something else by the time she comes home again.'

'So you're not going to ring that advice centre?'

'Not in the meantime. No point in making a fuss. Let's just sit tight and see what develops.'

Diane looked at him for a long moment. Then she stood up and left the room.

Gordon leant slowly forward and put his head in his hands.

Nina was reading Alice a bedtime story when her mother appeared in the doorway, her face stiff with disapproval.

'There's a phone call for you,' she said meaningfully.

'Oh—thank you.' Nina closed the book. 'I'll be back in a minute, darling.'

From her mother's face, she had no doubt who was on the phone.

'Daniel?'

'Hello, Nina. Are you doing anything at the moment?'

'Reading to Alice. Why?'

'Like to come out for a coffee?'

'Now?' It was nearly nine o'clock.

'Please, Nina. I've something to tell you.'

'All right,' she said, aware of her mother's rigid presence in the background. 'Fifteen minutes?'

'Fine. I'll wait at the gate so your mother doesn't have to see me.' There was rueful amusement in his voice.

Nina put the phone down and, not meeting her mother's eye, said lightly, 'I'm going out for a coffee. I don't suppose I'll be long, but I'll settle Alice first.' And she ran back up the stairs.

He was waiting in the car when, fifteen minutes later, she let herself out of the front door. He leant over to open the door for her and, taking her by surprise, gave her a quick kiss as she settled herself beside him.

'Where are we going?'

'The King's Head's as good as anywhere. Have you been in since it reopened? It's well worth a visit.'

Nina hoped no one she knew would be there, but her friends were more likely to be in the bar than the coffee lounge.

'We had a visit from the police this evening,' he went on as he turned the car into East Parade.

'What?' Her head spun towards him.

'The second in three days, actually—they came while

we were out on Saturday.' He gave a short laugh. 'It's all right, no one was arrested.'

Nina said carefully, 'What did they want?'

'The first time, according to Adam, they were asking about an old lady Lucy used to visit. This evening they were more interested in her son. He's the one who was murdered last week.'

All this because Lucy had called on Mrs Kershaw? Webb certainly had a bee in his bonnet. 'What's it got to do with you?'

'Nothing, except that his mother left us everything to us.'

She drew in her breath. The DCI hadn't told her that. How long had he known?

'And the police have only just found out?'

'It seems so. And you know the way their minds work.'

Indeed she did. She'd heard the missing solicitor had been located and was flying home. The Governor must have got it from him.

Daniel had turned into the car park behind the hotel. 'Anyway, they wanted to know where we all were when he was murdered. Charming, isn't it?'

Nina looked up at the precipice of the building towering above them, studded with lighted windows. Perhaps one of them had, this time last week, been Philip Kershaw's.

Daniel put a hand on her arm. 'Look, I only told you because I thought it would amuse you. Don't *worry* about it.'

'Were you all able to satisfy them?' she asked, forcing a light tone.

'Of course. Innocent as newborn babes, the lot of us. Right, let's get into the warmth; there's quite a nip in the air.'

He took her arm and led her into the hotel. Its change of ambience was immediately apparent, and Nina, suppressing her sudden anxiety, looked about her with interest. The corridor in which they found themselves was panelled in pale wood, with a moss green carpet. It looked very different from when her mother used to bring her for tea after visits to the dentist.

The lounge, opening off the corridor through a glass door, was even more of a transformation. People were relaxing in comfortable-looking chairs upholstered in apricot, while the lampshades and the large, ornamental jars which stood on the hearth were a striking turquoise. Over in one corner, a pianist was playing a selection of songs from the shows, and sets of watercolours hung luminously on the walls.

Daniel directed her to a two-seater sofa. The waiter glided up and he ordered coffee.

'My goodness!' Nina said, looking round the room. 'It's hard to believe it's the same place!'

'Yes, they've done wonders with it.'

'Out of the nineteenth century straight into the twenty-first!'

'Except,' Daniel said, 'that there isn't going to be a twenty-first century.'

Nina's heart jerked. 'Then it's a pity no one told them before they spent all those millions!' she said flippantly. She turned to look at him. His face was serious but the feverish glitter she'd noticed on Saturday was back in his eyes.

Hey! she thought. Watch your step, girl! 'You said you had something to tell me.'

'Yes—great news. You know the Captain's due this evening? Sarah and Brad have gone to Headquarters to meet him.'

'I did hear, yes.'

'Well, he's actually coming to Shillingham! We heard today that he's visiting all the UK groups while he's over, and he'll be here on Saturday, Nina, at Victoria Drive!'

She found the radiance in his face embarrassing and looked away, grateful for the tray of coffee which had been discreetly placed on the table in front of them. Its fragrant, everyday smell was part of a normal world which didn't take much notice of prophets and the coming of the Apocalypse. With a shaking hand she poured it and handed a cup to Daniel.

'And Brad particularly wants you to meet him. Normally, the Captain only sees officials, but you're so near to joining us and I think Brad hopes it will tip the balance.'

Nina remembered her reactions when the possibility had first been mentioned—her feeling of excitement and awe at the thought of meeting the founder of the Movement. Had it been only last week? Now, she was more ambivalent, not sure she wanted to expose herself to that dangerous, charismatic man.

More importantly, now the DCI was taking an active interest in the group, her conflict of interests had intensified. He should be told of Bellringer's visit; the trouble was that he'd ordered her not to see them again.

Not exactly, though, she defended herself. He'd said she must drop the investigation, and she had. The suggestion that she shouldn't go back had been only that, a suggestion. What she did in her own time and in a private capacity was surely no concern of the Chief Inspector.

Daniel said with a smile, 'Aren't you going to say anything?'

'I was just wondering if it's wise for the Captain to move about so openly in view of police interest in the Movement.'

Daniel laughed derisively. 'The police can't touch him.'

'Not unless he breaks the law, no. But—'

'Not even then.'

She turned to look at him. 'What do you mean?'

'Nina, the Captain is the Lord's appointed servant and answerable only to Him. No man can sit in judgement on him.'

Her mouth was suddenly dry. She forced herself to say lightly, 'The law might not see it that way.'

'Don't worry, my love, he's in no danger. In the unlikely event that the Devil's agents move against him, our contingency plans would go into action.'

'And what are they?' she asked fearfully.

'Look, stop worrying, will you? Nothing's going to

happen to the Captain, believe me; that's all you need to know. Now, pour me another cup of coffee, there's a love, and let's change the subject.'

Webb, replete with spiced chicken, was nodding over his papers when the doorbell rang, jerking him awake. It was Hannah.

'I saw the light under your door, or I wouldn't have rung,' she said apologetically, noting his bleary eyes. 'I got your message; sorry I missed dinner, but I hoped I might be in time for coffee and a liqueur.'

'Excellent idea. What time is it?'

'After eleven, I'm afraid. I've been at a Governors' Meeting and they tend to drag on.'

'I'm delighted to see you. I've had enough of my own company.'

Hannah sniffed appreciatively in the hallway. 'Whatever it was, it smells good.'

'Another time,' he said, filling the kettle.

She took mugs from the cupboard and watched him prepare the *cafetière*—he seldom produced instant coffee; like his disdain of the tin-opener, it was a matter of pride with him.

Webb carried the tray into the living-room, and Hannah noted the pile of papers by his chair. 'How are things going?'

'One or two interesting developments,' he replied, putting a small glass of brandy beside her mug. 'According to the solicitor, Mrs Kershaw left the bulk of her estate, in the region of quarter of a million, to the Revvies.'

'Good heavens! And her son?'

'Zilch. What's more, he didn't know the score till the day he died, when he visited the solicitor. It was stipulated in the will he must be told in person.'

'That must have been an incredible blow.'

'Yes. Anyway, on the strength of all that I went to beard the Revvies in their den. Come to think of it,' he added with a grin, 'one of them is called Daniel, at that!'

'What are they like?' Hannah asked curiously, kicking off her shoes.

'Butter wouldn't melt in their mouths. Helpful, friendly, all pals together. Four men and four women living in the house, all "tenants", I was told.'

'Were they paired off, or singles?'

'Hard to be definite, but taking personalities into account, I'd say they're separate entities. No married couples, at any rate, and I shouldn't be surprised if one of the men was homosexual.'

'Were they quite open about their inheritance?'

'Oh, yes. Furthermore, they made it plain that they're entitled to it, since they could do more good with it than anyone else—"saving souls", if you please. Still, we took the opportunity of noting their alibis for Monday lunchtime, which Dawson will start checking in the morning.'

'Anything promising?'

'Not really. Honestly, it defeats me, Hannah. A man and woman come quite openly into the hotel bar, collect Kershaw and go off with him, and they might have been invisible for all the notice that was taken of them. I mean, you'd think *someone* would have remembered them. Mrs French seems to be the only one who saw them at all, and that such a fleeting glimpse that she can't give any description. They've had the devil's own luck—they could hardly have counted on making so little impression.'

He sipped his brandy reflectively, appreciating the taste on his tongue, the mellow lamplight and Hannah's shadowed face opposite—the end of a long day. Time to relax, perhaps to make love.

He roused himself to say, 'What of your invalid?'

Hannah shrugged her shoulders. 'She was kept in the san over the weekend, but she's gone home today. She was determined to—John Templeton said that short of chaining her to the bed he'd no choice, though he's not happy about her.'

'And the young Revvie recruits?'

'Under observation, if I may borrow one of your phrases. Nothing else to report.'

'According to the evening paper, Bellringer's arrived in this country. That's all we need.'

'He's not an undesirable alien, then?'

'Not so far, but he, too, will be under a certain amount of observation. Discreet, of course.'

Hannah finished her coffee and put the mug on the table by the chair. 'I ought to be going.'

'Do you want to?'

She met his eyes. 'Now that you mention it, not really.'

'Excellent. I don't want you to, either.'

They made love slowly and unhurriedly, delighting in each other and the pleasure given and received. And Webb reflected, as so often on such occasions, how fortunate he was in this relationship, which made no demands and yet was so eminently satisfying. He'd been anxious, he remembered, that Hannah's acting headship might bring her into more frequent contact with Charles Frobisher. And with a sudden jolt, remembered she had spent the evening with the school governors.

'How did the meeting go?' he asked later, as they lay side by side in the darkness, drowsy and at peace.

'All right. As I said, it dragged on a bit, but things seem to be ticking over all right.'

'Frobisher there?' Webb couldn't refrain from asking.

'Of course, he's the chairman.' She paused then, taking the decision, added lightly, 'I'm going to the Golf Club Dinner with him on Friday.'

Webb's stomach knotted apprehensively. 'Are you indeed?'

'The Templetons will be with us.'

'As chaperones?' he asked nastily, and was grateful that she didn't reply. He reached contritely for her hand. 'Sorry.'

'You don't have to worry, you know,' she said gently. 'I'm fond of Charles as a friend, but that's all.'

'It's not all as far as he's concerned, as he made quite plain.'

'That was two years ago; things change.'

'Some things.'

'Would you rather I hadn't told you?'

'No, but I'd rather you weren't going. And before you say anything, I know perfectly well that you're a free agent. It's just that I like it to be me you're free with!'

She laughed softly. 'I was under the impression that I've just been exceedingly free with you!'

And she turned to face him as he pulled her back into his arms.

Across the town, Nina was also lying awake, though alone. Not that she need have been, if she'd played her cards differently, and it was this fact that kept her tossing and turning as she went over and over the events of the evening.

With hindsight, it would have been better not to have gone, but coffee had seemed innocuous enough. And, her brain reminded her brutally, she'd wanted to see Daniel, which wasn't innocuous at all.

She had, after all, been fully aware that he was attracted to her, and after two lonely years that was heady enough. Even so, he had taken her completely by surprise when, instead of taking her home, he had driven out to Chedbury Woods and parked under the trees. It was there, she remembered painfully, that she and Ross had done their courting.

Of course she'd protested when she realized they were going in the wrong direction, but he'd merely laughed and continued on his way. Then, as soon as he'd parked, he turned to her with an urgency she wasn't prepared for and to which, to her despair, she had found herself responding.

For long, breathless minutes time had fused, and in the shadowed car it could have been Ross who was holding her so tightly, whose kisses were becoming increasingly demanding. Then her clamouring body shuddered back to the present and in her head she heard Daniel saying, 'There isn't going to be a twenty-first century.'

She'd pushed him away from her, gasping as he continued to kiss her ears and throat. 'Stop it, Daniel—no!'

'What do you mean, no? It was very definitely "yes" a minute ago.'

'I'm sorry—I shouldn't have—'

'Why shouldn't you? We're both free. You're surely not trying to tell me you don't want it?'

Casting round for excuses, she said weakly, 'I'm sure the Captain wouldn't approve.'

He laughed. 'Outside marriage, you mean? Love is a God-given gift, Nina, and as long as it hurts no one, he's all in favour. After all, it's love that binds people together— one of the strongest ties there is.'

She resorted to cliché. 'I've been hurt once, I—'

'I shan't hurt you, Nina mine. I want to marry you and carry you off to my mountain top.'

Her instinctive recoil told her that the spell was broken and she was free again. She forced herself to say calmly, 'But we've only known each other a few days; it's much too soon for decisions like that. Now please, Daniel, take me home.'

There was quite a lot of arguing but eventually he'd given in, placated by her promise to think things over.

Which was what she was doing. For the first time in ten days she was thinking rationally about what had taken place and her own part in it. And what appalled her was her gullibility, especially when she'd been only too aware of the dangers. Thinking herself immune, she had blundered on, meeting the leaders socially, allowing Daniel to take his first, tentative kisses.

Hot with shame, she recalled her resentment when the DCI had expressed his suspicions—suspicions, moreover, which she herself had implanted. *Was* it all down to Daniel's blue eyes, or had some diluted effect of sublimation blurred her judgement? A combination, probably, since that was how they worked, appealing to the basic need to be loved, to be singled out as special. Her ego, bruised when Ross left her, had been soothed and flattered by the welcome she'd received—as, no doubt, had those of all the other 'converts'.

Whatever the reason, she had behaved less than professionally, and she bitterly regretted it. It was now up to her to repair the damage as best she could, and the first thing she must do was tell Webb of Bellringer's imminent arrival.

The fact that it was the name 'Bellringer' that came to her and not 'the Captain' was the final proof, were it still needed, that she had emerged on the other side of the experience. It was now up to her to rescue the others.

CHAPTER 13

'You're telling me that, despite my orders, you've continued to associate with them?'

The grey eyes were like gimlets. Nina held their gaze, though her face flamed. 'Only in a private capacity, sir. You told me to drop the investigation, and I did.'

'I was more specific than that, Inspector, chiefly for your own sake. You could have been in grave danger.'

'I realize that now, sir.'

For a moment longer he regarded her in silence, then he leaned back in his chair. 'Well, since you appear to be still in one piece, what have you to report in your "private capacity"?'

'Bellringer's coming to Shillingham, sir. On Saturday.'

Webb groaned. 'As if we haven't enough on our plate. To address a meeting?'

'No, only to see his followers. But they've invited me to go along.' She didn't meet his eyes.

'You *are* flavour of the month. You appreciate that now you've told me, I can stop you going?'

'I hope you won't, sir. It could be a useful exercise.'

'I have the suspicion, Nina, that you didn't escape quite as unscathed as you'd have me believe. If you go back again, you might fall right into their trap.'

'I've been inoculated now, sir. Really.'

'They've no suspicion you're in the police?'

'None.'

'Well, if you think you can help us put a spoke in their wheel . . . Did you hear they've inherited Mrs Kershaw's estate?'

'Yes, Daniel Stacey told me.'

'They've also ensnared a couple of schoolgirls from Ashbourne. Some cassettes and pamphlets came into our possession, and they're pretty powerful stuff.'

'I saw the girls my first evening, but I couldn't do anything without giving myself away.'

Webb tapped his desk with his pen. 'What worries me about that crowd is that while they seem harmless enough, they're like "sleepers", leading ordinary, blameless lives till they get the call to action. Then, believe me, they can become lethal. I've seen it happen.'

She said quietly, 'I know; they think they're above the law and can evade it if necessary. And I'm quite sure they'd die for Bellringer, without thinking twice.'

'Exactly. And I don't want you dying with them.'

She smiled slightly. 'There's not much chance of that. I've behaved stupidly, sir, not taking sufficient account of what I was doing. I'm sorry. I promise that it won't happen again.'

'Very well; if you really want to go on Saturday, you have my permission. But for God's sake, be careful.'

It was at the pedestrian crossing in King Street that Christina saw her, a young woman in a fitted grey coat, pushing a pram. She watched without interest as she crossed in front of the car, but suddenly the woman's profile and the way she held her head tweaked at her memory. Surely there was something familiar about her?

Christina frowned, trying to remember. Who was she?

Where had she seen her before? Somewhere, she felt certain. The memory tantalized her, and she stared after the young woman as she continued along the pavement, until an impatient toot from behind recalled her to her surroundings and she reluctantly moved on.

Probably a client, or someone she'd met at a party. Yet she had the odd feeling she'd never actually spoken to the girl. No doubt it would come back to her, she told herself and, seeing an empty parking meter, slid thankfully into it and gathered her swatches together for her next call.

At break that morning, Mattie sent for Stephanie and Marina on the pretext of handing over some set books. She was trembling as she waited for them to arrive. It had taken several hours of a sleepless night to steel herself for such a meeting and only terror at the thought of the Prelate's displeasure had finally goaded her into it.

Although expecting them, she jumped when they tapped on the open door.

'Good morning, Miss Hendrix,' they chorused dutifully.

'Come in and close the door. Now, I've managed to get you some cassettes. They're a little more advanced than those you had, but all the Initiate ones are out on loan.'

She paused, surveying their eager faces, and forced herself to add, 'Have you any questions or difficulties you'd like to discuss?'

'We just wish we could get to the meetings,' Stephanie said. 'It's a pain having to miss them—everyone else will be ahead of us.'

'Not everyone, a lot of people can't get there. That's why we have the tapes, so you can keep up.'

She hesitated again. 'Has Miss James said anything more to you?'

They shook their heads.

'We'll just have to hope it's blown over, then. But be very careful with these new tapes; if you're caught with them, you'd have to explain where you got them.'

Marina said curiously, 'Doesn't anyone here know you're a Revelationist, Miss Hendrix?'

'No one.'

'I should have thought you'd want to tell everyone and get them to join, too.'

Out of the mouths of babes . . . Mattie smiled stiffly, repeating the excuse she had made to Brad. 'I should, I know, but I find it hard to speak of things that matter deeply to me.'

They nodded with apparent understanding and she felt a surge of affection for them. 'Have you heard the Captain's coming to Shillingham on Saturday?' she asked on impulse.

'Coming here? The *Captain*?'

'That's right, to Victoria Drive.'

'And you'll actually meet him?'

'I very much hope so.' Did she? When he might well denounce her and take away her chance of salvation?

'Oh, please let us come!' Stephanie begged.

Mattie was startled. 'You know that's not possible.'

'But if you gave us permission—'

What had she started? Mattie thought, panic-stricken. Whatever had possessed her to mention the visit?

'Now that's enough. Off you go to break, and take good care of those tapes.'

As they left the room she bowed her head and waited with closed eyes for her agitation to subside sufficiently for her to continue with her timetable.

The following morning, Webb received a summons to Constabulary Headquarters at Stonebridge. He'd been expecting it.

'Sit down, Spider.'

The nickname had been invented years ago by an old lag and taken up by Webb's colleagues until he'd made clear his dislike of it. It was no longer used in his hearing except by the Chief Super, with whom he could scarcely argue and who invariably addressed him by it.

'Now—' Fleming cocked his head on one side as was

his wont. 'Fill me in on what's happening with this hotel murder.'

'We're going full out on it, sir,' Webb replied, 'but no definite lead has emerged as yet.'

Fleming pulled at his lower lip. 'The deceased was resident in France, I believe. Does that narrow the field, or widen it?'

'We've been unable to establish any feuds or resentments over there. He gambled, but always paid his debts and was respected in his home area.'

'Happily married?'

'It would seem so.'

'Right, well, talk me through the case, will you?'

Webb did so, sketching in the Revvie connection when he came to it with some apprehension. It was not misplaced. Fleming interrupted him at once.

'Who exactly are these johnnies?'

'One of the New Age religions, sir. They believe there's going to be a second Flood and they'll be the only ones to survive it.'

'And the victim's mother believed all that tosh?'

'They're pretty convincing, sir.'

Fleming snorted, waving a vague hand. 'Carry on, then.'

This time Webb was allowed to proceed without interruption until he had completed his account.

'And this mysterious couple haven't resurfaced?'

'No, sir. It's amazing how completely they've vanished from the scene.'

'There's no clue at all as to who they might be?'

'None. As far as we're aware, Kershaw knew no one in the area. We checked with the Revelationists, on the slim chance that he might have met them, but their alibis have been checked and seem to tally. In any case, since they'd got their hands on his inheritance it was Kershaw who had the motive, not the other way round.'

Fleming nodded gloomily. 'Well, don't drag your feet on this one,' he said in dismissal. 'Top brass are getting restive; they're looking for a quick result.'

Then perhaps, Webb thought acidly as he took his leave, they'd be good enough to tell him how to achieve it.

'I don't know what's got into Miss Dilys,' Peggy Davis commented to her husband when she returned to the kitchen with her employer's supper dishes.

'She's sitting at the table staring into space, and her plate scarcely touched.'

'Well, she's in the middle of a book, isn't she?' Bob returned without looking up from the racing results. From long experience, that simple fact explained a multitude of things.

'But she's not getting on with it, is she? She just moons about looking out of the window and wandering round the room. I've seen her from the garden, when I've been hanging out the washing. As for that writer's block, as she calls it, when she went to the library on Monday I thought she was over it.'

'It's my opinion the nanny and baby are unsettling her,' Bob pronounced, relighting his pipe. His wife paused in her act of scraping the uneaten food into the bin.

'You might be right, at that. There's no doubt she's taken against Nanny Sarah for some reason. I can't think why; she's quiet enough, goodness knows, not a bit of trouble. And Seb's an angelic baby. I wasn't looking forward to them coming, that I do admit, but I'll be quite sorry when they go.'

'Well, I reckon Miss Dilys won't, and no more will I. Might have a bit of peace in the evenings, without you jumping up and down like a shuttlecock to check on the baby because that girl's out again. Hardly ever in, if you ask me. I reckon you should be getting a quarter of her wages, minding it nearly every night.'

'Go on with you!' Peggy said, but she smiled shame-facedly and added after a moment, 'You don't really mind, do you, Bob? Me being a bit taken up with the baby?'

He reached up and caught her hand as she passed. 'Lord love you no, that was only my fun. If you want to spend your time gurgling and cooing over the young 'un, you go straight ahead, girl! No skin off my nose.' And, giving her hand a little squeeze, he returned to his paper.

Christina said suddenly into the darkness, '*I* know who she was!'

Edward stirred sleepily. 'What?'

'The woman I saw in King Street yesterday. It's been niggling at me ever since. She's the one who was with that man at the King's Head.'

Edward came fully awake. 'Are you sure?'

'Positive. I should have realized before.'

'It could be important, then.'

'Yes; I'll ring the police in the morning.' She gave a little shiver. 'What's happening to us, Edward? First the murder, and now these awful people turning Stephie against us.'

He slid an arm under her shoulders and drew her close. 'It's just a bad spell we're going through, sweetheart. We'll come through it all right, as long as we have each other.'

But for the first time he wondered uneasily if that was, after all, quite enough.

The phone sounded and Webb reached for it, glad of the interruption.

'Chief Inspector? It's Christina French. I thought you'd like to know that I saw that woman on Tuesday—the one who left the bar with the man who was murdered.'

Webb tensed, leaning forward. 'On Tuesday?' he repeated sharply. Two days ago; why the hell—?

'Yes; I'm sorry for the delay, but I couldn't remember where I'd seen her. It only came to me in bed last night.'

'Go on, Mrs French.'

'Well, that's it, really.' She sounded slightly deflated. 'She crossed the road immediately in front of me, pushing a pram.'

'You're sure it's the same woman?'

'Positive. I recognized her at once, though as I said, it took me some time to place her.'

'Can you describe her for me?'

'Early to mid-thirties, quite tall, straight figure, wearing a tailored grey coat. No hat. Mid-brown hair, caught back with a tortoiseshell clip. Pale face. That's about it.'

'Excellent. I wish all witnesses were as precise. And the pram?'

'One of the high, old-fashioned kind—Silver Cross, I think. White, with a black hood.'

'Could you see the baby?'

'I was concentrating on the woman, but it must have been several months old, because it was sitting up.'

'And where exactly was this?'

'At the pedestrian crossing in King Street.'

'Which way was she walking?'

'Towards Westgate.'

'The time?'

'Just before ten-thirty; I was on my way to an appointment.'

'Well, that's very good news. The size of the pram seems to indicate that she's local—she couldn't have come in a car, for instance. No sign of the man waiting further up the road?'

'I didn't see him.'

'I'm much obliged to you, Mrs French. Thanks for phoning—we'll be in touch.'

He slammed the phone down and shouted through the open office door, 'Ken, Bob, Harry—in here at the double!'

The three detective sergeants arrived within seconds, slightly out of breath.

'A positive sighting of the woman suspect at last.' Webb reeled off the particulars Christina French had just given him.

'Bob, get on to all the Pram Clubs, Young Wives' Groups, crèches, clinics, etc., and see if they recognize the description. If you don't have any luck, move on to doctors' surgeries and, if necessary, maternity units at local hospitals. The birth could have been anything from three to twelve months ago. Get a handful of DCs to help you.

'Harry, organize a team to cover all the shops in King Street with the same description, particularly chemists and those selling baby clothes or toiletries. This could be the break we're waiting for, lads. If she's still around, she must live locally and, contrary to how it's seemed so far, *someone* must know who she is. On your bikes!'

The two sergeants hurried off, leaving only Ken Jackson awaiting orders.

'And you and I, Ken,' Webb finished, getting up from his desk, 'are going back to the King's Head. Armed with that description, we'll interview all the staff again, and as many of the guests from last week as we can track down. She doesn't look like your normal bar customer and someone might have noticed her. Apart from the conference delegates, I imagine much the same crowd goes there every lunch-time. Perhaps at last we can jog someone's memory.'

Hannah sat at her dressing-table brushing her hair and wishing she could summon up a little more enthusiasm for the evening ahead. The Frenches were sure to be there, which, if they were still sulking after last week's interview, could be awkward. Lord knows, she hadn't wanted to antagonize them, but for Stephanie's sake plain speaking had been essential.

She was also apprehensive of Charles's attitude. Though she'd assured David any closeness between them was in the past, there had been occasions, some quite recent, when, turning suddenly, she had caught Charles looking at her in a way that left no doubt about his feelings for her. All in all, she heartily wished she had declined his invitation.

The doorbell rang, and she gave her reflection in the mirror a rueful smile. Such misgivings were far too late; the evening was about to begin.

The entrance to the Golf Club was directly opposite Hassocks, and Hannah glanced at its lighted windows as Charles slowed down, remembering that the self-contained young woman who was staying there knew Miss Hendrix.

Had she been more approachable, Hannah might have enlisted her help.

Then the car turned into the gateway, Hassocks was behind them, and Hannah put her concerns behind her as well, determined not to allow any nebulous worries to spoil her evening.

The clubhouse was an imposing building, single-storeyed but with high, raftered ceilings and panelled walls. As they walked through the door into the lounge hall, they were immediately caught up in the social chat and laughter of a group of people determined to enjoy themselves.

Charles excused himself to fight his way to the bar, and Hannah looked about her, recognizing several faces among the crowd. Then she heard her name called, and turned to see the Templetons approaching.

They were a charming couple, Hannah thought, as she smiled a greeting: John so tall and straight with his thick grey hair and gentle, reassuring manner; Beatrice—Gwen's elder sister—rounded and still pretty, with Gwen's large, vulnerable brown eyes.

'Hannah, dear, how nice!' she said now, leaning forward to exchange kisses. 'I'm so pleased we're sitting together. Have you heard from Gwen recently?'

'Last week, yes. She's having a wonderful time.'

'And how about you? Coping all right?'

'We've had our moments, as John might have mentioned.'

'My dear, John never mentions *anything*. Discretion itself—most frustrating!'

Charles joined them, handing Hannah her glass. 'Greetings, everyone. Have you studied the seating plan?'

'Yes, we're on table eleven.'

'Who's with us?'

'The Donaldsons, the Perrys and the Frenches, if I remember correctly.'

Murphy's Law, Hannah thought with resignation. She was confident, though, that the Frenches' social graces would rise to the occasion—and with luck they might be at the far end of the table.

Various other people joined their group, and in the clamour of voices it became increasingly difficult to make oneself heard. Hannah was relieved when the Club Captain rang the bell and requested everyone to take their places for dinner.

'How's your mother?' she asked Beatrice, as they filed into the dining-room. Old Mrs Rutherford, who normally lived with Gwen, was staying with her elder daughter while she was in Canada.

'Quite well, really. Her cataracts are troubling her, but John says she's not ready for an operation yet.'

The Frenches were already standing behind their chairs—as Hannah had hoped, at the opposite end of the table. They smiled and murmured pleasantries as she passed them. Then applause broke out as the Captain and his guests made their way to the top table, grace was said and there was a general scraping of chairs as everyone sat down. Hannah gave a sigh of satisfaction and picked up the menu.

In his flat at the top of Beechcroft Mansions, Webb wondered moodily how the evening was going. For all Hannah's denials, he felt sure Frobisher hadn't given up hope of winning her round. Well, there was damn-all he could do about it.

What he *could* do was get out his sketch pad and see if he could make any sense of this baffling case. At least they were making some progress. Following Mrs French's phone-call yesterday, he and Jackson had met with more luck at the King's Head; the description of the wanted woman had indeed struck a chord, and one man, a regular lunch-time customer, recalled bumping into the trio in the doorway of the bar.

'Yes, I remember them now,' he'd said. 'Sorry—I didn't realize it was them you were interested in; the description you circulated earlier rang no bells, but I remember the woman, and the other bloke who was with her, tall and thin. They were coming out of the bar as I was going in and we literally collided. The bloke said, "Pardon me", and I registered that he was American.'

Webb's interest had quickened. 'Are you sure?'

'Well, that's all he said, but he had an accent, and an Englishman would have said "I beg your pardon" or just "Sorry".'

'Can you describe him for us, Mr Bennett?'

The man shrugged. 'As I said, he was tall and thin—looked very intent and serious as he came out, which is probably why he didn't see me—but he was pleasant enough when he apologized. Long face, bony forehead—you know the type.'

'Dark? Fair?'

'Nondescript—brown hair. I didn't notice the colour of his eyes. Nothing special about him, really.'

As Webb recalled the conversation, he was making a quick identikit-type sketch of the man as described. It was a stroke of luck he was American—should make him easier to trace. Since the woman had a baby it was on the cards that they were married, in which case she might also be American. And bearing in mind that, in view of the large pram, she probably lived locally, inquiries were already under way for an American couple in the vicinity.

He began to sketch her—drawn-back hair, tall, pushing a pram. Then he sat back and studied the drawing. A rather plain young woman with a baby. What in heaven's name was her connection with Philip Kershaw?

Whom Webb turned to next, a few quick lines of his crayon making him instantly recognizable. After a moment, he added the phone box in King Street. Had Kershaw made a call to the couple from there, and if so, how had he known them?

He dropped the first sheet of paper to the floor and, taking another, embarked on a series of vignettes, lifelike caricatures of the group of Revvies. Strictly speaking, their only relevance in the case was Mrs Kershaw's bequest, but they'd earned a place in his deliberations.

When he had drawn everyone connected with the case, Webb began the second stage of his operation. This involved focusing his attention on each in turn of the faces he had depicted, attempting to pierce through the public mask to the nature of the person behind it. Had any of them lied? If so, why? And which, if any, was capable of murder?

Engrossed as he was, the sudden shrill ringing of the telephone made him jump. Swearing softly, he put down his crayon and went to answer it.

The Golf Club dining-room was large and handsome with a gallery at one end. Beneath this, honours boards listed in gold the names of past captains and competition winners, and a glass-fronted trophy case displayed silver cups and salvers.

Despite her earlier reservations, Hannah was enjoying herself. The soup had been excellent and she was now pleasurably awaiting the guineafowl which was the main course.

It was at that point that a waiter approached John and touched his arm. 'Dr Templeton? You're wanted on the telephone, sir.'

John frowned. 'But I'm not on call this evening. My partner, Dr Fellowes—'

'It's Dr Fellowes on the line, sir.'

Without further protest John excused himself, pushed back his chair and hurried out of the room.

'That's odd,' Beatrice commented, 'Malcolm never contacts John on his free evenings. I hope nothing serious has happened.'

That it had was obvious on John Templeton's return as, grave-faced, he quietly asked Hannah and Charles to accompany him outside.

Threading her way between the tables with Charles close behind her, Hannah was conscious of a hard knot of apprehension. What dire news could the phone-call have contained to necessitate this grave summons from the dinner table?

In the deserted lounge, cut off from the warmth and gaiety of the diners, they turned anxiously to John.

'Bad news, I'm afraid,' he informed them. 'Hannah, my dear, I'm so sorry—it's Miss Hendrix. She appears to have taken her own life.'

Minutes later, having arranged with the Donaldsons to take Beatrice home, they were in John's car driving to the police station. Hannah sat in the back gripping Charles's hand. She was very cold and her mouth was dry. All she could think was: *It's my fault. I should have prevented this.*

'She'd an appointment at the surgery this evening,' John said, breaking the silence as they waited at traffic lights. 'Just a check-up, which I'd made a condition of allowing her home. She didn't keep it, so, knowing I was concerned about her, Malcolm went along there after surgery. She's not on the phone—there was no other way of contacting her.'

The lights changed and they turned into Leyton Road. 'There was a light in her window, but though he knocked and rang there was no reply. So, by then extremely worried, he got on to the police, who broke in.'

I don't want to hear any more, Hannah thought, and yet I must. I have to know how she died, even though the picture of it will stay with me always.

She said with an effort, 'Was it—an overdose of some kind?'

But John couldn't enlighten her. 'I don't know, Malcolm didn't go into details.'

They turned into the gateway of the police station and skirted the grass and lily-pond to draw up at the front steps.

Hannah suddenly realized where they were. 'Why have we come here?' she asked, as Charles got out and held the door for her.

'They need to ask questions,' he said gently.

'God, Charles, I didn't understand. *Why* didn't I realize how desperate she was?'

'Hush now, it's all right. You've nothing to reproach yourself for.'

They went up the steps and through the swing-doors into the brightly lit foyer. John went over to the desk and explained to the sergeant on duty who they were.

'DCI Webb's still at the scene, sir. If you'd like to wait in one of the interview rooms, I'll have some tea sent in.'

The next hour was a merciful blur. They sat facing each other across the small table, and the green walls were reminiscent of a hospital waiting-room. The tea was hot and strong, served in polystyrene mugs. Hannah thought of her glass of claret, still on the table at the Golf Club. It seemed a different world.

Though the radiator under the window was on, she remained cold, encased in her private misery. How could she explain this to Gwen? How would it affect the school? All points to be considered, though the overriding consideration was the tragedy itself. Poor, poor woman, to be driven to this.

Then, at last, David came, with the little ginger-haired sergeant she'd met before. And though all she wanted was to go to him and bury her face in his jacket, she could only sit and gaze helplessly up at him.

Webb nodded at the two men, both of whom he'd met previously, and gave Hannah a brief, perfunctory smile. 'I'm sorry to have kept you waiting. Now, Miss James, I believe the deceased was a member of your staff?'

Hannah moistened dry lips. 'That's right.' Her voice croaked and she cleared her throat and added for the sake of clarity, 'Yes.'

'Were you aware she was also a member of the Church of the Final Revelation?'

Hannah gazed at him dumbly, feeling her eyes stretch wider and wider as further complications presented themselves.

'Who the devil are they?' asked John Templeton.

'A New Age cult who have taken up residence here.'

Hannah said in a whisper, 'I'd no idea. None.' She turned to Charles. 'You remember I mentioned them at the Governors' Meeting.' And added for John's benefit, 'Two fifth-formers went to one of their meetings a fortnight ago. They were given tapes and pamphlets—'

'There was a supply of them in Miss Hendrix's bedsit,' Webb interrupted, 'as well as a selection of more advanced cult literature. Also some kind of thesis she was working on. Do you know anything about that?'

Hannah shook her head. It seemed her ignorance was total.

'It was headed "The Gospel according to Matilda" and seemed to be an account of her religious experiences and interpretations of the scriptures.'

'My God!' Charles said under his breath—aptly, thought Hannah, fighting down hysterical laughter. 'It must have been she who involved the girls.'

'It's possible, sir, though the meeting had been well publicized. There was a sealed letter addressed to a Prelate Lübekker at No. 5, Victoria Drive. Does that mean anything to you?'

They all shook their heads.

Well, it bloody does to me, Webb thought: it means there are more of those devils around than the ones we interviewed last Saturday. Which could be very significant.

More questions followed, to most of which Hannah could give only negative answers.

'Had the deceased—Miss Hendrix—seemed under any kind of strain?' David asked finally, and she almost laughed.

'She was *always* under a strain! She hardly ate a thing, lived on her nerves. And no doubt I added to her troubles,' she ended shakily. 'About ten days ago, I took her to task for dressing shabbily.'

Charles said quickly, 'You couldn't know.' Then, to Webb, 'Miss James and I discussed this, and it was I who persuaded her to speak to Miss Hendrix, try to get her to smarten herself up. To be frank, she dressed like a tramp, though she'd a good salary and no dependants as far as we knew.'

'Her money would have gone to the sect,' Webb said flatly. 'They're always extorting it from their members for one reason or another.' Nina had told him that.

'You allow them to carry on like this?' Frobisher demanded.

'They're not breaking any law, sir. If they do, we'll be ready for them.'

He turned to John Templeton. 'Now, Doctor, I believe the dead woman was your patient? Could you explain the circumstances in which you last saw her?'

Hannah barely listened as John went through Mattie's collapse and confinement in the sanatorium.

'I didn't want to discharge her,' he ended, 'but she was adamant. In the end, I agreed on condition that she took things easy and called in at the surgery this evening for a check-up.'

Webb nodded. 'Perhaps you'd be good enough to identify her before you leave. She's at the mortuary.'

It seemed the interview was at last over. David had closed the file in front of him, the ginger-haired sergeant his notebook. As they all rose to their feet, Hannah, moistening her lips, asked, for the second time, 'Was it an overdose?'

Webb hesitated, glancing at her white face, then shook his head.

'Well?' Charles prompted, impatient on Hannah's behalf for his reply, yet unsure how she'd react to it. 'May we know how she died, Chief Inspector?'

Webb said levelly, 'She was found hanging from the banisters.'

Hannah made a small sound and Charles's arm went protectively round her. He was still supporting her as, in shocked silence, the three of them left the interview room. Webb looked after them for a long minute. Then he turned to Jackson.

'OK, Ken,' he said wearily, 'it's after midnight—I think we can call it a day.'

CHAPTER 14

Jackson said gloomily, 'I'm just sorry for the Governor, that's all. He's got enough problems without his young lady playing him up.'

Millie refilled his cup. 'Come on, love, I'm sure she wouldn't do that.'

'That's what it looked like, coming in all dressed to the nines, with that other bloke in tow.'

'She wasn't there from choice,' Millie said reasonably. 'Who is he anyway, this man she was with?'

'Name of Frobisher. Something to do with the school, I think.

'What's he like?'

Jackson grinned. 'What you'd call a smoothie. Talks posh, natty dresser.'

Two-year-old Tessa banged on the tray of her high chair and Millie hastily supplied another slice of toast.

'Anyway, all I'm saying is when they went off with his arm round her, old Spider looked as though he'd been pole-axed. And I couldn't say anything, because he's firmly convinced no one knows about his little arrangement.'

'Well, no one does except us,' Millie said comfortably, 'and we wouldn't split, would we? Poor Mr Webb, though. I hope it works out for him.'

Nina learned of Mattie's death when she arrived at her desk that morning and immediately went to see Webb.

He looked up from his papers and she was struck by how tired he looked. Probably been up half the night, she thought with quick sympathy.

'I've just heard, sir. About Mattie.'

He nodded. 'We were called to the apparent suicide of

a schoolmistress. It wasn't till Bob took a look round her flat that he realized she was a Revvie and gave me a bell.'

'She was a teacher, was she? I didn't know that.'

'Head of English at Ashbourne, no less.'

Nina looked startled. 'Then she must have been responsible for inviting the girls, though I never saw her with them.' She paused. '*Was* it suicide, sir?'

'We'll have to wait for the PM results. On the face of it, though, I'd say that's the most likely bet, though of course it could have been rigged.' He looked up at her. 'With hindsight, would you consider her a potential suicide?'

'I never spoke to her, so I couldn't say. I thought she looked odd, but that was all. She was one of those on the stage at the meeting—a Gospeller.'

'Yes, we found her gospel. Enough to put the fear of God into you.'

'Perhaps that was the intention,' Nina said.

Webb rubbed a hand tiredly across his face. 'Quite probably. What did strike me is that this Hendrix woman wasn't around when we went to the house. Are there any others who live locally but not actually at Victoria Drive? A Prelate Lübekker for instance?'

'I've met him, but he's based in London. There's Sarah, though—I think she's local. She doesn't live at the house, but she spends a lot of time there.'

'Surname?'

'Sorry, sir, they don't usually bother with them.'

'Any idea where she works?'

'Afraid not.'

'There's not an American couple with a baby, by any chance?'

'Not as far as I know.'

Webb sighed. After a moment, he said, 'Do you still want to go along this afternoon?'

'Certainly. Apart from anything else, it'll be interesting to see how they handle this.'

'What time are you going?'

'Twelve o'clock. A buffet lunch, I gather, then a pep-talk-cum-prayer meeting. It'll probably go on till about four.'

'All right, I'll give you a clear run, though we'll need to see them again. Even if murder's ruled out, we have to make sure it wasn't a suicide pact. Still, we can start with the school and see what we dig up there.'

He'd also have to see Hannah, Webb thought as Nina left, and the sooner he got that over, the better.

Suiting the action to the thought, he pushed back his chair and strode from the room. 'I'm going out, Ken,' he announced, pausing at Jackson's desk on his way through the outer office. 'The PM's at eleven-thirty but it should be pretty straightforward. All being well, I'll meet you in the Brown Bear at one and we'll take it from there. In the meantime you can get up to date on last night's report.'

Hannah was not at her flat, and only after he'd stood for several minutes pressing the bell did it occur to Webb that she would have gone to the school. Which showed how sluggishly his brain was working.

At Ashbourne, several cars were parked in the drive. He wondered sourly if one of them was Frobisher's. His ring was answered by a subdued woman, who conveyed him along the corridor to Hannah's study.

She rose as he came into the room and he saw that she was pale and her eyes were circled with shadows. To his relief, there was no sign of Charles Frobisher. The picture of them leaving the interview room with his arm around her had stayed with Webb as a permanent backdrop to all the other worries of the night.

'Hello, David,' she said quietly. 'Have there been any developments?'

'Not really. The post-mortem's in just over an hour; we'll know more then.'

She gave a quick frown. 'There's some doubt over how she died?'

'It has to be formally established.'

'Then could you let me know the result, please? As soon as possible?'

'Of course. It'll be necessary to interview some of your staff, I'm afraid—those who came into regular contact with her. And possibly some of the girls.'

'Only the house-staff are here over the weekend, and most of them didn't know her. But the matrons might be able to help; they looked after her last weekend.'

'What about the teaching staff? Can I contact them?'

'They live all round the town, but I can give you the addresses of those most closely involved with her.'

There was a tap on the door and the secretary came in with coffee. As she was leaving, Hannah said, 'Amanda, would you list the addresses of the English Department, please? Mr Webb will need to interview them.'

'Certainly, Miss James.' She turned to Webb. 'If you call at my office when you leave, I'll have it ready for you—it's the next door along.'

'I suppose all this will be in the papers?' Hannah said, as soon as they were alone again. 'I've already spoken to the house-staff and boarders. I had to do it at once, or the most terrible rumours would have started. Though what could be worse than the truth—'

She broke off, biting her lip. Webb said quietly, 'I really am dreadfully sorry, Hannah.'

'Then there's Gwen,' she went on, as though he hadn't spoken. 'God knows what I can tell her—though John and Beatrice might already have been in touch.'

'Hannah—'

She looked up then, meeting his eyes. 'I've got to live with this, David.' Her voice shook slightly. 'I can never forgive myself for adding to her problems. Perhaps if I'd been more understanding, tried harder to find out what was worrying her—'

'Be logical; she's hardly likely to have killed herself because you asked her to dress more smartly.'

'It might have been the last straw.' She paused, looking down at her hands clasped on the desk. 'I suppose it was naïve of me, but I rather hoped you'd have looked in last

night, when you got home. I could have done with some
moral support.'

'I thought you already had it,' he said, before he could
stop himself.

'I see. Well, yes, Charles was very understanding, certainly.'

'I wouldn't have wanted to butt in.'

She said steadily, 'I'm not sure what you're implying,
David, but if it's that he spent the night with me then you're
mistaken. When we got home he poured us both a brandy
and sat with me until I'd got over the first shock, and then
he went home.'

It was not necessary to add that her state of shock had
involved a horrendous shaking and, finally, the relief of
tears, when Charles had held her gently and kissed her
hair. It would have been easy, she thought now, for him to
have pressed his advantage, but he had not done so and
she was inordinately grateful. It was not his fault that she
would rather it had been David who was there to comfort
her when her need was so great.

Webb said in a low voice, 'I didn't think that, not really.
I'm sorry, Hannah, I'm behaving like an oaf. I'd better
go.'

She nodded, not sure if she could hold her composure,
but as he reached the door she said impulsively, 'Nothing's
changed, you know. After last night, I mean.'

It was a badly needed reassurance. 'Bless you,' he said
softly, and let himself out of the room.

Only as Nina reached Victoria Drive did it occur to her
that the community mightn't yet have heard of Mattie's
death. Certainly the police hadn't notified them.

However, she'd no time to plan any strategy. The door
was immediately flung open by Daniel, who caught hold
of her hand and drew her inside, kissing her soundly on
the mouth. Apparently there were no hard feelings about
the other evening.

'The Captain's arrived,' he announced excitedly, 'and he's looking forward to meeting you.'

He shepherded her ahead of him into the meeting room, now restored to its full length. A long table with a buffet set on it stood against the far wall, and two or three smaller tables with chairs were dotted about.

Then Nina caught sight of Noah Bellringer, and Mattie was instantly forgotten. A huge, bear-like man with a shock of silver hair, he was standing halfway down the room surrounded by an admiring group. His deep, mellifluous voice seemed to draw her towards him, and she had actually started down the room even before Daniel took her arm to lead her to him.

Brad, who had his back to them, turned at their approach, and smiled at her. 'Ah, here she is! Captain, this is Nina, whom we've been telling you about. Since she's almost family, we included her in the party.'

'Of course.' With the full impact of Bellringer's attention on her, it was an effort not to quail. As he took her hands in his own huge ones, a powerful current vibrated between them, almost painful in its intensity. Faith healers produced the same effect, Nina told herself, vainly attempting to constrain this powerful personality within acceptable bounds.

'Sister Nina, welcome—welcome! And this is Brother Dwight, my faithful friend and assistant.'

'A High Priest,' Daniel whispered in her ear, as the tall, black-bearded man next to Bellringer smiled and bowed.

Annabel was approaching with a tray of glasses, half of them filled with red wine and half with white, and Nina felt obliged to take one. She'd no intention of drinking it, even though it was unlikely to be doctored at this gathering of committed members; she needed a clear head to answer Bellringer's searching questions without betraying herself. It was a relief when someone came up to speak to him and she was able to move away.

Looking round the room, it seemed she was indeed the only 'outsider'; this visit must be to encourage the faithful, not to increase their number. Had anyone noticed Mattie wasn't here, or didn't they care? Certainly no one seemed worried; there was a buzz of electricity in the air, compounded of excited anticipation and a kind of exaltation—just the volatile mix, Nina thought uneasily, which could prove dangerous.

People were beginning to move towards the buffet table, and Lucy and Liz had taken up their places behind it, ready to serve the food. It was a tempting display: delicious-looking salads, lasagne, chilli bean casseroles, bowls of rice and vegetables. It was several minutes before Nina realized that neither meat nor fish was on offer.

She carried her plate over to join Ruth and Vince at one of the tables and was about to sit down when there was a sudden, urgent ringing of the doorbell, followed immediately by a fusillade of knocks.

The chatter of conversation died suddenly as everyone looked at each other. Nina went cold. The DCI had promised her free rein; what could have gone wrong?

'I'll go,' Adam said into the silence, and a dozen pairs of eyes followed him out of the room. The sound of young, excited voices reached them, then he reappeared in the doorway accompanied by the two schoolgirls from Ashbourne. This was it, then. Nina held her breath.

Bellringer's powerful voice boomed across the room. 'Well, Brother Adam, who have we here?'

'These girls are Initiates, Captain. They've come with some disturbing news. It seems that Mattie—Sister Matilda—has taken her own life.'

For several timeless seconds no one moved. Then the tall, fair girl came forward into the room and approached Bellringer.

'We were told this morning, sir. It's horrible—no one knows what to do. But we thought you ought to know, so as soon as we got the chance, we slipped out.'

She looked up at his kindly, concerned face. 'Please, Captain, don't send us away. I know we shouldn't be here but we so wanted to meet you.'

He put a hand on her shoulder. 'Bless you, child, of

course I shan't send you away. You're more than welcome at our gathering.'

It was too much for Stephanie; the strain and excitement of the last week, the news of Henny's death and the unbelievable fact of being face to face with the Captain finally overcame her and she burst into tears.

Annabel moved forward and put an arm round her.

'But Sister Matilda has no need of your tears,' Bellringer was continuing. 'She is today in Paradise with the Lord. We must rejoice that she has found peace.'

Nina dragged her eyes from him to see how the others had reacted. Sarah'd slipped her hand into Brad's but her face was impassive, as was his. Daniel was standing rigid and white-faced by the buffet table, and, behind it, Lucy's face was streaming with tears.

The second schoolgirl now moved into the room with Adam, and Vince stood up to greet her. Normal conversation was starting up again, responding to the Captain's assertion that grief was inappropriate. In any case, Nina suspected that apart from soft-hearted Lucy, it was shock they'd experienced rather than genuine grief.

She moved her chair to make room as Terry and Vince brought both girls to the table and introduced them to her and Ruth. She wished very much that they weren't here, so directly under Bellringer's powerful influence, but at least she'd be able to keep an eye on them.

Back in his office after lunch, Webb's thoughts returned to Hannah. He'd promised to let her know the result of the PM. Although it would have complicated matters, he almost wished he could assuage her guilt by telling her it had not after all been suicide. Well, delaying it wouldn't help; she'd probably be home by now. Reluctantly, he lifted the phone.

'Hannah? I'm ringing with the post-mortem results, as promised. There was nothing to suggest anyone else was involved in Miss Hendrix's death.'

There was a brief pause, then she said quietly, 'Thank

you.' After a moment she added, 'What about the other case? Are you any nearer tracking down the killers?'

He was relieved at the change of subject. 'Possibly a little. We now have the descriptions of the couple who left the bar with Kershaw: a plain woman in her thirties and a tall man, probably American. Mrs French saw the woman on Tuesday, pushing a pram in King Street, so with luck—'

'A pram?' Hannah interrupted sharply.

Webb straightened in his chair. 'What is it, Hannah?'

'Could I have that description again?'

Puzzled, he gave it to her in more detail, reading from Christina French's statement in front of him. 'Early to mid-thirties, quite tall, mid-brown hair caught back with a tortoiseshell clip, pale face. And she was pushing a large white Silver Cross pram with a black hood.'

'Sebastian's,' said Hannah unsteadily. 'My God, it must be.'

'Must be what?' Webb demanded urgently. 'And who the devil's Sebastian?'

'The baby that's staying with Dilys. And the woman is his nanny, David! The description fits exactly!'

Webb said incredulously, 'You're telling me you know her?'

'Yes, it's Sarah Baines. And she has an American boyfriend, Dilys said, though I don't know his name. God, David, does that mean—?'

'Have you got Dilys's phone number?' Webb interrupted, reaching for his pen.

Shakily, Hannah gave it to him, then he heard her gasp. 'David, I've just thought! I saw her in the town one day, talking to Miss Hendrix. She might belong to the cult, too!'

Nina had mentioned a Sarah. 'She might indeed. Bless you, Hannah—it looks as though we're almost there. I'll get on to Dilys now—Miss Hayward, isn't it?—and with luck we can go straight round and nab the woman.'

But there his luck ran out. Dilys, bewildered by his circumspect questions, informed him that Miss Baines had gone out for the afternoon and she wasn't sure what time she'd be back. Webb apologized for disturbing her and hung up, suddenly knowing where she would be: meeting Noah-bloody-Bellringer. With Nina.

For several minutes Webb sat staring in front of him. It was damnable that Nina should be there in the thick of it, unaware of this latest development. Was there any way, without endangering her, that her presence could be made use of?

No, he decided almost at once, it was too risky. As it was, he'd have to underplay his visit. He'd been there before; they weren't to know this time was any more serious. Then, once inside the house, he could extract Nina before arresting the couple.

He pressed the intercom. 'Come in, would you, Ken. We have a tricky one here.'

At Victoria Drive lunch was over, the tables cleared, and the main purpose of the day had begun. They'd swivelled their chairs to face the dais, where Bellringer, his second-in-command and Brad Lübekker had taken their places. The Captain was now, as Nina thought with inward amusement, in full flow.

However, at the moment he had less than her complete attention. Probably as a result of the chilli, she had developed a raging thirst and was becoming desperate for a drink of water. The Captain had been speaking for twenty minutes already and showed no signs of stopping.

Surreptitiously, she looked behind her. Her chair was only feet away from a door leading into the corridor. As unobtrusively as possible, she let herself out of the room. It was doubtful whether, held in thrall as they were, anyone saw her go.

She found herself at the far end of the corridor, opposite the room where drinks were served before meetings and just short of the kitchen.

The latter was, of course, deserted, but with a touch of the *Mary Celeste* about it, since all the surfaces were covered with dirty plates, glasses and cutlery, and a pyramid of pans filled the stone sink. Obviously, whoever was on kitchen duty had deferred the washing-up till after Bellringer's departure.

Nina located a clean mug and, reaching across the pans, filled it at the sink, where she drank long and luxuriously of the ice-cold water, looking out of the window as she did so.

It was not an inspiring view; the back garden was small and scrubby, any plants having long since given up the unequal struggle and abandoned it to weeds. As in most houses of its age, a gate in the far wall gave access—doubtless the old tradesmen's entrance—and a rickety shed stood alongside. The only colour in the entire landscape was provided by the washing line, which flaunted a pair of jeans, several socks and a pink nylon nightdress flapping disconsolately in the breeze. A plastic bag of pegs, Nina saw, hung on the back door.

Her thoughts turned to the two girls: had they come from home or from school, she wondered, and hadn't anyone missed them? And how was she going to extricate them from Bellringer's spell without exposing herself as a police officer?

She should be getting back to them. She rinsed and dried her mug, replaced it on its hook, and returned to the meeting room. Not a head turned as she entered. She crept unnoticed to her seat and, after a quick glance at the girls' wrapt faces, returned her attention to the Captain.

Hannah stood, telephone in hand, staring unseeingly at the wall in front of her. She said explosively, 'That just isn't possible!'

The house-mistress's frightened voice reached her over the wire. 'Honestly, Miss James, I don't know what to say. Marina came to my study soon after you'd spoken to us. She said Kathryn Stuart had invited her and Stephanie to lunch and Miss Fowler had given permission. I admit I was distracted, still shocked about Miss Hendrix. It just never occurred to me to check.'

'But you *know* those two have to be closely watched at the moment. Even if they *had* been invited to Austen, they should have been accompanied there and back.'

'I realize that. I can't apologize enough.'

'Apologies,' Hannah said crisply, 'are of singularly little use at the moment. There's nothing for it, we'll have to contact their parents and see if they've gone home.' Which would mean admitting that the school's supervision of the girls had proved no more effective than their parents'.

A fact which neither family failed to draw to her attention. Smarting under their comments, though well aware they were justified, Hannah attempted to smooth things over.

'Please don't worry. It's quite possible they're still in the grounds somewhere—we're looking now.'

'A waste of time!' Gordon Chase stormed. 'It's damned obvious where they've gone—back to those infernal God-botherers. And I for one am quite prepared to go round and dig them out.'

Hannah was alarmed, particularly in view of the suspicions now centred on Sarah Baines. 'Mr Chase, I must ask you most strongly to do nothing of the kind. It could cause exactly the kind of incident we must avoid.'

'What incident? What's wrong in a father calling for his daughter?'

'We don't know how they'd react. Please, I really must urge you to leave it to the police.'

'You're getting on to them?'

'Yes, if we don't find the girls within the next few minutes.'

'Then what *can* we do, for God's sake?'

'Wait by your phone. We'll contact you the minute we have any news.' And she hung up on his further protestations.

'Once more unto the breach,' Webb said under his breath as their car turned into Victoria Drive, closely followed by Bob Dawson's with a couple of DCs in the back. As arranged, Dawson stopped just round the corner, two houses short of No. 5.

'OK, Ken. Let's hope we can get this cleared up with the minimum amount of bother.'

They walked up the path, climbed the steps, and rang the front doorbell.

Once again its ringing sounded through the room, coming, fortuitously, in the middle of a dramatic pause in the oration. For a moment no one moved. Then Bellringer said, 'This is not a time for interruptions. Can you see who it is from the window, Brother Daniel?'

Daniel, who was at the table nearest the front of the room, went to look, lifting the net curtain. He let it fall, and turned back to face them all.

'It's the police,' he said.

Nina's heart jerked. But he'd *promised*! Something unexpected must have happened.

'They've been before,' Daniel added. 'I shouldn't think it's anything serious.'

'Is there an intercom?'

'Yes, sir.'

'Then I suggest you use it rather than opening the door.'

Daniel went into the hall and they heard him say, 'Yes?' And then, 'Yes, she is, but it isn't convenient to speak to her at the moment. We're in the middle of a meeting; could you come back later?'

Nina's nails dug into her palms. Was it she the DCI wanted? Should she offer to go out to him? But then they'd wonder why he wanted her, might even try to stop her, and her cover would be blown. She hesitated in an agony of indecision, but prevailing caution kept her in her chair.

The one-way conversation seemed to be developing into an argument and she grew steadily more uneasy. With an exclamation of annoyance, the Captain stepped down from the dais and strode up the length of the room to the hall. His voice reached them clearly.

'This is Noah Bellringer. I must ask you to leave—you're

interrupting our meeting. If you wish to speak to someone here, you can call back later.'

A pause, then: 'And what, might I ask, is so urgent that it can't wait another hour?'

In the meeting room the small group sat unmoving, ears straining so as not to miss a word of the disjointed conversation.

Bellringer spoke again, and his voice had hardened. 'Since you refuse to explain, I can't help you. But I repeat, this door will not be opened until our meeting is finished. And please don't attempt a forced entry. We have two young girls here—I should not like any harm to come to them.'

The veiled threat was not lost on Nina, and she closed her eyes on a wave of nausea. Oh, no! Not a hostage situation! God, what could she *do*?

'Names?' Bellringer repeated, obviously to Daniel, and then, into the intercom, 'Stephanie and Marina . . . My dear sir, I have no intention of sending them out. They came here of their free will and here they'll stay.'

Nina reached out a hand to Marina, sitting rigidly beside her, and felt her responding grip. It seemed that her complacent resolve to keep an eye on the girls could prove more hazardous than she'd anticipated.

CHAPTER 15

Out on the doorstep, Webb stood motionless, his heart like lead. Was it a bluff about the girls? Should he make an immediate forced entry before they could marshal their resources? Nina was inside, but they didn't know she was planted—she should be safe enough.

He turned as DC Marshbanks appeared at the gate and came running up the path. 'A message on the radio, Guv. Ashbourne School have reported two of their girls missing, Marina Chase and—'

'Stephanie French,' Webb finished with him, as all hopes of a quick end to the siege evaporated. It was true, then.

'They think they might be at this address,' Marshbanks added, hiding his surprise that the Governor should know of them.

'Thanks, Simon. Unfortunately, a hostage situation has developed. Arrange for BT to immobilize the line—we want total isolation here. Ken, radio HQ and get them to inform the ACC of the situation. Ask for back-up and tell them I'll contact them shortly.'

As he spoke he was hurrying back down the path, the two men at his heels. Jackson stopped at their car and Webb ran along the pavement to Dawson's. Seeing him approach, the sergeant got out and waited apprehensively on the pavement.

'Bad news, Bob—possible siege. You and Trent get round the back on the double—there's an access road behind—and keep watch in case they make a dash for it. I'm asking for back-up and reinforcements.'

Inside the house Bellringer and Daniel came back into the room and returned to their places. Daniel looked shaken, but the Captain's anger had given way to a palpable excitement. It was as though he'd had a fix, Nina thought, and was on a high. He glanced down at Sarah, seated below him, and gave a slight nod. Then he surveyed the rest of them, his face alight with zeal.

'My friends, the forces of Satan are gathering against us. We cannot allow them to prevail.'

There was an uneasy stirring among his audience. His glittering eyes moved from one table to another, searching their faces. Nina, her heart knocking against her ribs, avoided his gaze.

'Brothers and sisters, the supreme test is upon us— earlier, I admit, than I'd hoped, but it is not for us to question our destiny. We are required only to submit, joyously and with faith.' He took a handkerchief from his pocket and wiped it across his face. 'Shortly, a stupendous choice will be offered you, but first it is only right you should be told the reason for this sudden crisis.'

Everyone waited, unmoving.

'As you know, our time has always been short and we've had much to do. It follows that we could not afford setbacks. If doubt is planted in people's minds, valuable time must be wasted in removing it, and prevention is better than cure.

'You know also that in certain circumstances the Elders of the Movement are above the law, answerable only to that Authority which is higher than all others. If we do evil for our own ends, it is right we should be punished; but if in doing the Lord's will we should go against laws that are man-made, we remain blameless.'

He paused again, surveying them as though awaiting some kind of challenge to his statement. None came. Even without subliminal help, Nina noted, he could hold his audience in the palm of his hand. However deluded, he was indeed a charismatic leader.

'Under extreme conditions, therefore,' he continued, 'we are empowered to execute any person who, by threatening us or hindering our work, might cause serious harm to others. Better one death than thousands.'

Kershaw!, she thought, with a flash of understanding. It had to be.

'And it was this dilemma that, a few days ago, faced Prelate Lübekker. Step up here if you please, Brother— and Sister Sarah with you.'

He waited for them to join him. Sarah was even whiter than usual and there was a nerve jerking in her throat. Beside her, Brad stood like a rock, staring down the room above their heads.

'You are aware,' Bellringer went on, 'of the generous legacy left us by Mrs Kershaw, which will speed up the building of our Salvation Cities. You will also have read of the death of her son, here in Shillingham. Sister Sarah, you were the first to become involved. Will you take over, please, and explain what happened?'

Nina longed for her recorder. If only she'd thought to bring it!

Sarah started talking in a low voice which nevertheless carried clearly throughout the hushed room. 'On Monday last week I called in here towards lunch-time with a note of my new phone number—I was moving to Lethbridge Road the next day. While I was in the study the phone rang, and as soon as I lifted it a man at the other end started ranting and raving about our stealing his inheritance, and threatening to "expose" us to the tabloids.'

She paused and moistened her lips. 'I'd no idea who he was or what he was talking about. At that stage, none of us knew Mrs Kershaw had a son. Fortunately, at that moment Prelate Lübekker came into the room and I passed the phone to him.'

She stopped and turned to Brad, who took up the story. 'The caller was extremely agitated and I couldn't get any sense out of him. It was clear, though, that we couldn't simply hang up, because there was no knowing what he'd do; so I arranged for us to go to the King's Head, where he was staying, and meet him in the bar.'

He looked down at the riveted, upturned faces. 'As the Captain said, sometimes it is necessary to take the law into our own hands. We couldn't afford scandal, especially just then; the Captain's arrival was imminent, and his visits to towns all around the country have been highly promoted. The last thing we wanted was sensational stories in the press.

'Another factor was that whoever this man claimed to be, we needed the money we'd been left—quite legitimately, let me stress. In fact, quite a proportion of it had already been allocated. Having weighed all these points, we took with us, as a precaution only, the means of silencing him if all our reasoning failed.

'As, sadly, it did. He was in no mood to listen and just kept accusing us of undue influence. So we suggested going to his room to discuss the matter more privately. Though we still hoped to talk him round, our main concern was to avoid a scene in the bar, which was becoming increasingly more likely.

'But we did no better up there. No matter how often we explained, he kept insisting he'd take us to court and inform the press of what he called our shenanigans. So in the end we had no choice.'

Brad looked again at his motionless audience. 'I must emphasize that no one in this room except ourselves and the Captain here knew what had happened. We hoped we could have kept it that way.'

Adam's voice, strained and highly pitched, asked, 'So what happens now?'

It was Bellringer who answered. 'Now, Brother, there are choices to be made. Somehow the police have learned of our involvement, and by this time, no doubt, the house will be surrounded—I expect a voice over the loud-hailer at any minute. Realistically, we can only hold them at bay for a limited time.

'Regarding Sister and the Prelate here, I mentioned that only in extreme cases is extreme action taken. But once it *is* taken, if things go wrong that action must be followed through to the end.'

'You'll hand them over to the police?' That was Daniel.

'No, Brother. It is not seemly that men should sit in judgement on those who do the Lord's work, and provisions have been made accordingly. When need be, the right of execution may be extended to oneself. Our brother and sister here will avail themselves of that right, answering for their actions not to the police but directly to that higher Authority.'

He felt in his pocket and Nina went cold as he extracted several small foil sheets.

'In wartime, tablets such as these were issued to spies behind enemy lines. Our war, against Satan, goes on.'

'Suicide pills,' said Terry under his breath, and Stephanie gave a choked little cry.

'Death will be painless and instantaneous, my friends, you have my word on that. The moment the police break

into the house, Sister Sarah and the Prelate will each swallow a tablet.'

His face was now shining with a radiance that Nina found
terrifying. 'Do we want our brother and sister to journey
alone?' he demanded exultantly. 'Or shall we be willing
fellow-travellers? Naturally, I myself shall be accom-
panying them; there is no way the forces of evil shall get
their hands on this servant of the Lord!'

There was an uneasy stirring in the room as, against
their will, his followers felt the pull of his suggestion.

Bellringer's eyes, mesmeric and compelling, circled them
again. 'Think, brothers and sisters! Today you too could
be in Paradise, free to do the Lord's work without the fetters
of this mortal flesh. Naturally, those who prefer to face the
police may elect to do so. But what a glorious gesture a
mass exodus would be! What a testament to our faith!'

Moving to the small table on the dais, he tore the foil
sheets into separate squares and, with great deliberation,
laid them out in a row. Then he stood back and lifted his
hands, inviting all who wished to come and take one.

'No more worry and hardship,' he said softly, 'no
violence, terrorism or cruelty. No loneliness or pain. No
fear of the unknown, for all will be clear. The peace of it—
ah, the peace!'

Sarah turned and, walking like an automaton, went to
the table, took a foil-wrapped pill, and stepped down from
the dais. Brad followed her. Rigid in her chair, not breath-
ing, Nina waited. If one moved, they all would. *Please, no!*
she willed them desperately. *Stay where you are, for God's sake!*

But after a timeless pause Adam pushed back his chair,
and with a slow, ceremonial tread walked to the dais and
picked up a foil square. A lesser pause, then Daniel followed
him. Around her, chairs were beginning to be pushed back.
A multiple tragedy was being set in motion. She could wait
no longer.

Victoria Drive was cordoned off and neighbours warned to
stay indoors. A rendezvous point had been established in

the forecourt of the Cock and Feathers in Lethbridge Road, where Webb had passed on his knowledge of the situation to senior officers and briefed the back-up teams as they arrived.

The original anxious group, composed of the Frenches, the Chases, Hannah and Charles, had been joined at the police barricade by a steadily growing crowd who had stopped out of curiosity, persistently ignoring the uniformed constables who tried to move them on.

Behind parked cars and garden walls the firearms team had taken up their positions and cameras were trained on the inscrutable frontage of No. 5. The air crackled as different groups communicated by radio. Hannah could see David talking to the tactical firearms officer. Further down the road, Superintendent Donaldson was conferring with the negotiator. The immediate action plan had been agreed on and operations were about to begin.

She would collect a pill, Nina decided. The lab would want to analyze it and there might even be a chance of an antidote, though if death was as instantaneous as Bellringer had said, that was unlikely. Following Ruth, she went to claim her right to die, her brain moving into top gear.

The pills wouldn't be taken till the police broke in—that was the plan at the moment. Therefore they must be warned of the situation.

Returning from the dais, she saw that Stephanie and Marina were preparing to go up in their turn. Nina stopped and put a hand to her head, and, as she'd hoped, they paused.

'Are you all right?' Marina asked anxiously.

Disregarding the banality of the question in such circumstances, Nina replied, 'I feel a bit faint. Could you—come with me to get a glass of water?'

'Of course.' Marina took her arm and for a moment it seemed that Stephanie would continue to the dais. Quickly, Nina swayed against her so that the girl instinctively caught her and the three of them, barely noticed, went out into the corridor.

Even before the door had closed, Nina, taking them unawares, had caught hold of each girl and was running with them through the kitchen to the back door.

Pushing back the bolts, she said swiftly, 'Now get out as quickly as you can and *run*.' No doubt the authority Brad had recognized in her came to her aid—that and the fact that the girls were used to discipline. For whatever reason they made no demur but obediently started through the door.

As they emerged, several heads rose above the level of the back wall and the gate swung open. A man moved cautiously into the gap and, after a moment's assessment, beckoned them.

Pushing the girls in front of her, Nina ran towards him. 'DI Petrie. Can you come in straight away—quietly and from the rear? They're planning mass suicide the minute you appear, but they're expecting the loud-hailer first.'

'I'll get straight on to Control. How many are in there?'

She calculated rapidly. 'Twelve. They're in the room on the right, most of them seated at tables. There are two doors, one further up the passage—it'd be as well to come through both simultaneously and go straight for the foil squares they're all holding. I don't think anyone's armed. Now hurry, for God's sake. I'll go back and do what I can.'

And before he could remonstrate she had turned and run back into the house.

When Nina slipped back into the room, they were all sitting with bowed heads while Bellringer led them in prayer. No pills seemed to have been swallowed yet, but the Captain, possibly tiring of the police's waiting game, was obviously building up to it.

'Your people are desirous of being with you, oh Lord!' he was intoning. 'We have saved many souls following your divine inspiration, and others will continue our work here on earth. We pray you will receive us this day to work more

closely with you for the salvation that is at hand. Even
now—'

Nina moved silently up on to the dais. 'Wait!' she said
loudly, startling them all. Bellringer swung to face her, the
bowed heads jerked upright.

'Let us first give thanks for all the good things of life,'
she improvised wildly. (Would they be in position yet?)
'Let us remember the love of family and friends and pray
they will not grieve too deeply for us.' She hoped that message would go home.

'Let us give thanks for birds and flowers and all wild
things, for good food and fellowship, for sunshine and rain.'
It was an amalgam of school grace and 'All Things Bright
and Beautiful' she thought hysterically as she plunged
ahead, intent only on delaying the final, deadly act.

'Sister Nina—' Bellringer boomed, and she saw dawning
mistrust in his eyes.

'Please, Captain! I want to pray for my mother and my
little girl—'

There was a muffled sob from one of the tables.

Bellringer said angrily, 'That's enough! We go forward
joyously, regretting nothing! Brothers and sisters—'

And they were there at last, a dozen silent men
materializing among them, each aiming for a particular
target and searching out the lethal tablets. In a few cases
they were too late, but Nina, thankfully stumbling from the
room, did not learn that until later.

'So what happens to them now?' Hannah asked. It was
several days later and they were sitting in her dining-room
over a celebratory dinner.

'It's in the hands of the CPS. Baines and Lübekker are
behind bars on a murder charge and the rest of them
detained on bail while a report's made.'

'But what can they be charged with?'

'There could be conspiracy charges concerning the murder. And there are three more dead, remember; it's an
offence to aid and abet suicide.'

'Surely that applies only to Bellringer?'

Webb shrugged. 'It'll all be looked into, though I doubt if we'll proceed against the rest of them. But if Bellringer and that henchman of his are found guilty, they could get up to fourteen years.'

He refilled their glasses. 'It's a messy business all round, but it would have been a great deal worse without Nina. It's been tough on her, though, since she knew them socially. What of your errant girls?' he added. 'Will they need de-programming?'

'I don't think so; I suspect the final trauma did the trick. One good thing, their parents will pay more attention to them in future. I just wish we'd been in time to save Miss Hendrix.'

'Some people are natural victims,' Webb said reflectively. 'It sounds as though she was one of them.'

'What about Victoria Drive?'

'If they're freed from bail they'll move out, and if they're charged it'll be closed down. Either way, it's the end of the Revvies as far as Shillingham's concerned.'

'Well, that's certainly worth drinking to,' Hannah said.

Nina lay in bed, grieving for the waste of life she'd been unable to prevent; for Daniel and Adam and gentle Lucy, all of whom had harmed no one. If anyone had to die, she thought rebelliously, why hadn't it been Bellringer, or Brad and Sarah who, after all, had killed Kershaw? So many deaths, and all because one old lady had disinherited her son.

She let her mind drift back over the last two weeks, remembering the warmth and fellowship which, with whatever ulterior motive, had certainly been offered to her, the meal round the kitchen table, the laughter. Why could it not all have been as it seemed, without those dangerous undercurrents?

She was filled with a helpless hatred of Bellringer for his manipulation of those trusting souls who had followed him. What would Daniel's grandmother be feeling now—grief,

bewilderment, a total lack of comprehension which, perhaps, she had always felt towards him?

And Lucy's parents? Nina's hands clenched, knowing
how murderous she would feel if anyone harmed Alice.
Suddenly she needed to see her, to reassure herself that the
child was safe from the threat to which Nina herself had
unthinkingly exposed her. The memory of that day in the
hills, and the shadow coming over the sun, was still very
potent.

She slipped out of bed and went quietly to her daughter's
bedroom. Alice lay asleep on her back, her hair all over the
pillow and a copy of *The Borrowers* face down on the floor
beside her.

For several long minutes Nina stood looking down at her,
filled with a tumult of love and thankfulness. Then she bent
and slowly kissed her forehead.

It was over, they were both safe, and tomorrow was
another day. With which philosophical thought she went
back to bed.